A Three Rivers Holiday Tale

A Shifters of the Three Rivers novella

Kira Nightingale

Éditions Spottiswoode

Book Cover by 100 Covers

Edited by Brigitte Billings

Published by Éditions Spottiswoode

First edition 2024

ISBN (ebook): 978-1-998510-13-9

DEDICATION AND TRIGGER WARNINGS

Dedication

To my fabulous ARC and Street Teams – you guys are awesome! Thank you so much for all your support and encouragement. This one is for you! And an extra special shoutout and huge thank you to Jessica Earnest for coming up with the name Lark, and Adrienne Lozano who named the Knox Pack – for me, having names help shape the characters and Packs as I write them, so this book really wouldn't be the same without the names you came up with!

Trigger Warnings

This book contains some adult themes and lots of spice. There are characters dealing with grief in this story.

CONTENTS

Chapter One

MAI

My foot whistled past his head, less than an inch from his perfect fucking jaw.

He grinned at me. "You missed, baby."

No shit.

I snapped my leg back and then drove it forward into his solar plexus.

"Oof." The air was knocked out of his lungs as he stumbled back. I pressed my advantage, aiming for his head again—this time with a roundhouse kick. Too late, I saw the wicked glint in his eyes and felt the jolt of satisfaction pulse through our bond.

He darted toward me, catching my leg with one hand as his other hand snaked around my waist. Picking me up, he took two quick steps and slammed us into the gym wall.

Fuck!

Ryan had baited me, and I'd walked straight into it. My hormones were putting me on edge. I knew that, but I'd dismissed Ryan's suggestion that it was going to cost me in a fight. Only now, he and I both had proof of it. When he asked me to join him this evening in the new gym he'd installed at the Alpha House, I'd known what he was planning but I'd been so sure that I could handle it. But it had been way too easy for Ryan to wind me up and for me to stop thinking. I'd just wanted to wipe that cocky grin off his face, and instead, he had me pressed up against the wall, his whole body caging me in.

I licked my lips, feeling the heat from his body against me, his legs between mine. And that was the other thing these hormones were doing to me. I would go from angry to horny like the flick of a switch.

Ryan lowered his eyes to my lips. "Nuh-huh. No distracting me, Mai. We need to talk."

"After," I breathed huskily, rolling my hips and pressing my breasts into him.

Yes, I was using every trick I had. So sue me; I was horny as hell, and Ryan was everything I wanted.

"Mai." Ryan's voice held a hint of warning.

My eyes widened, and I looked up at him as I whispered, "Are you saying you won't fuck m—?"

His mouth crashed into mine before I could finish. Part of me felt smug that I could do this to him; the other part didn't care. She only wanted him inside of me. Now.

I broke the kiss, pushing him back just far enough so I could yank off his clothes.

I don't know if Ryan needed this as badly as I did or if my need was driving his through our bond, but he had me stripped of my clothes and completely naked before I could get his shirt off.

"Turn around," he ordered. "Hands on the wall."

I obeyed immediately. Hell, I'd do anything just to feel him moving inside of me. I could hear him stripping off, and it only made me wetter.

He kicked my legs apart and lightly trailed his fingers across my hips and ass.

This was taking way too long. "Ryan!"

"You know, I didn't think it was possible for you to get any more impatient, but I stand corrected."

I glared at him over my shoulder. "Either you do this now, or I'm getting my vibrator."

Ryan laughed and tweaked one of my nipples. "You threw it away, remember."

Shit. I did throw it away when we moved in to the Alpha House together. He knew my threat was empty. He had me exactly where he wanted. Panting and desperate.

"Ryan, please," I begged this time.

"Keep your hands on the wall."

His hands went to my hips, tilting them back to give himself access. Then he pushed inside of me. His cock was so wide that he had to ease it in, stretching me inch by slow inch until he filled me completely. It felt fucking delicious.

"This what you want?"

I threw my head back, just reveling in the sensation of him everywhere inside of me. "Yes, Goddess, yes!"

"Whatever my Alpha wants ..."

His fingers gripped onto my hips, holding me steady and using me to anchor himself as he teasingly pumped out and in.

I could feel my juices running down my legs already. How did I get so turned on by him? Even after all these months, it still felt like the first time. He consumed me, body and soul, and I couldn't get enough of him.

He set a rhythm that was neither fast nor slow but a steady pace designed to build my orgasm with each stroke. He knew exactly what I needed, and he gave it to me, thrusting his cock deep inside of me, then pulling out so only the tip remained before thrusting inside once again.

I knew I wasn't going to last long. I never did these days, but Ryan would draw it out as long as possible for me.

The cool air in here brushed over my naked body, making me shiver with the sensation as the gym faded away. All I could focus on was the overwhelming sensation of Ryan filling me, his scent surrounding me, and the pleasure coursing through me. In that moment, all I wanted was Ryan. All I could think about was Ryan.

"Faster, please, Ryan!"

"Whatever my Alpha wants," Ryan repeated, his fingers digging into my hips.

I moaned, the sound filling the room as he increased the pace, taking me to the edge and then pulling back, his control driving me crazy. I needed him to lose it, to pound into me uncontrollably.

"Please, please," I begged, my voice hoarse and desperate. I arched my back and tilted my hips, giving him more access, opening myself up to him, willing him to take it.

I felt the restraint in him snap. With a rough growl, his thrusts became wilder, more primal as he surrendered to the desire burning between us.

"Oh, Goddess!" I cried, my fingers digging into the padded wall as I met his ferocious rhythm.

"That's it, baby," Ryan grunted, his hips pounding into me. "I want you to come all over my cock."

His words sent me over the edge, my body convulsing around him as I shattered into a million pieces. I felt him shudder with his own orgasm, his hot cum exploding inside of me. It was incredible, delirious, delicious. I wanted to do this again and again. For it to never stop. I didn't want to deal with being an Alpha or being pregnant right now. I just wanted Ryan to make me feel like this for the rest of the night.

Ryan's thrusts slowed, and then he gently eased himself out of me. I almost whimpered, wanting to feel him inside for a bit longer.

He chuckled, knowing exactly what I was thinking. Then he turned me and pulled me to the floor.

I collapsed against him, panting heavily.

He pushed my hair from my eyes and kissed the tip of my nose.

"Feeling better?"

I sighed, snuggling closer to him. "Mmmm. For now."

"Oh, I'm not nearly done with you. But we still need to talk."

Not this again. "No, we really don't," I whispered sleepily.

"Mai, this is important. You're—"

"It's just the hormones, Ryan. It'll settle down."

He went silent for a moment, and I knew he was trying to work out how to say something without me losing it. "It's not just the hormones. You're restless and wound up all the time. Ever since you found out you're pregnant. Are you ... do you not want to be a mother? I know we didn't talk about having kids, I know you weren't ready, I know you're scared about the deal I made with the Dark Goddess ..."

"Ryan, stop, you're rambling!" It was so out of character for him, it was almost cute. "It's not that I don't want to be a mom. You're right; we didn't talk about it before. If we had, I would have said that I do want kids, but not for a while. I wanted to be settled first, with you, with the Pack, with being an Alpha. It was a surprise, that's all. I've had no time to get my head around the idea of me being a mother."

"You'll be a great mom, Mai."

I felt the tears welling up in my eyes. "You don't know that. I never had any younger brothers or sisters. We don't have cousins. I don't know the first thing about being a parent, Ryan. You, you practically raised your brothers. You know what to do. Me? I don't have a fucking clue! What if I'm awful? What if the baby hates me? What if I can't get it to stop crying all the time? What if I can't protect it when it needs me? What if—"

"Shush." Ryan's hand cupped the back of my head. "Now you're the one rambling. Is that what this is all about? You're scared you won't be good enough?"

"No! Yes ... I don't know." I pulled away from him, wrapping my arms around myself. "It's not just about being a good mother. It's about being a good Alpha, too. What if I can't be both? I might need to put being an Alpha above being a mother. How will a child understand that?"

"Mai—"

"No, listen. Ever since I found out I was pregnant, everything feels ... different. You're right. When I fight, when I make decisions, I don't think anymore. I just act on instinct. And I don't know if I should listen to it or fight it. What if I do that when the baby is born, and I do something wrong?"

Ryan pulled me closer and trailed his fingers down my back.

"You're going to be great. You kick ass as an Alpha, and you're going to kick ass as a mother. Everything else, we'll work out. We always do."

I closed my eyes. I wanted to believe him; I really did. But I couldn't help an overwhelming feeling that I didn't have a fucking clue what I was doing these days.

Chapter Two

MAI

Finally. Peace and quiet.

I curled deeper into the couch, tucking my feet under Ryan's thigh as I cradled a mug of hot chocolate topped with a mountain of marshmallows. Gremlin, our tiny white kitten, was sprawled across my lap, purring. Ryan had built a fire, and the flames cast a warm glow across the living room of the Alpha House.

"You know Derek's probably going to call any minute," I murmured, though I desperately hoped I was wrong.

Ryan's hand squeezed my ankle. "He won't if he wants to keep breathing. I made it very clear that unless there is a house that is literally burning down, we're not to be disturbed. We've earned this break, Mai. The Pack's stable, the territory's secure, and Derek can handle anything else that comes up."

He was right. We'd been running ourselves ragged since the battle with Brock, trying to prove to everyone that the Three Rivers Pack was safe under our leadership. Every day brought new challenges—integrating Korrin's rogues, dealing with Brock's former enforcers who'd surrendered at the Pack Meet, navigating the delicate balance of power with the other local Packs.

And then there was Jem.

My chest tightened at the thought of my brother. Jem's wolf still couldn't stand to be near me, not since I'd killed Hayley. The bond between us felt stretched thin, fragile. He was trying—we both were—but every time his wolf caught my scent, I could see the way he tensed, fighting against his instinct to attack. Jem's wolf blamed me for his mate's death, and his wolf hated to be around me. I was struggling to come to terms with my new relationship with Jem. When I ran away from the Three Rivers four years ago, after Ryan had rejected me in front of everyone, I'd bounced from city to city; I'd been alone, without a Pack, without family. I'd desperately missed my brother. Then, when I returned, after everything that me and Ryan had fought for, everything that had happened with Brock, I'd thought that I had finally got it all back. Instead, with his wolf urging him to attack me each time he saw me, it felt like I'd lost my brother all over again. Jem kept his distance from me now; to protect me, yes, but it still hurt like hell. Ryan knew how much I was struggling with it, and last week had a blazing row with Jem about it. They were arguing a lot these days, about the Pack, about the decisions we were making as the new Alphas, about me. I hated it; hated seeing them at each other throats. They'd been best friends for as long as I could remember. Neither of them thought I knew about their latest fight, but Esme had filled me in on all the details. Ryan wanted Jem to spend some time with me. Jem refused. Esme had said there'd been shouting. A lot of it. I wanted my brother back, but maybe him not being part of my life was something I was going to have to accept.

At least Jem had Esme. Esme was a witch, the first who I knew of to be part of a werewolf Pack, and I'd be lying if I said it wasn't an adjustment for all of us having a witch here.

After our parents died and Jem got together with Hayley, he'd been so busy working his way up in the Pack hierarchy and plotting to take over from Oliver, that he'd left raising me to Hayley. To say she wasn't interested in looking out for me was a massive understatement. I knew that guilty Jem felt about that; he'd told me himself when I came back. I got the impression that he felt Esme was a second chance for him. He loved her like a sister and looking after her was giving him a purpose again.

I liked Esme. She was just as protective over Jem as he was over her. Jem had been Alpha here for four years, used to being the one to make the decisions, to being obeyed without question. Ryan and I were the Alphas now, and it hadn't been an easy transition for him or the Pack. As a Pack, we needed a clear hierarchy. But no one was entirely sure who they should obey, and it made them uneasy when Jem was around. Jem could feel it in the Pack bonds, and it chewed him up that his own Pack felt that way about him now. Of course, then Esme picked up on it, and for a shy girl, she had no problem telling people off because of the way they made Jem feel. Loudly and repeatedly.

"Stop." Ryan's voice was gentle but firm, and I knew he could sense where my thoughts were taking me through our mate bond. "It's just us today, remember?"

I managed a small smile. "Right. Sorry."

He set down his coffee and pulled me closer until I was practically in his lap. Gremlin made an indignant sound at being displaced.

"Two days," he murmured against my hair. "Just us. No Pack

politics, no family tensions, no emergencies, no territory disputes, no—"

A loud knock echoed through the house.

Ryan's growl vibrated through his chest. "I'm going to kill Derek."

He lifted me up and gently set me on my feet, then he strode to the door, murder in his eyes. I followed him, hoping this was something we could sort out in thirty seconds and then get back to cuddling.

But when he yanked open the front door, it wasn't Derek standing there.

It was Wally, pink-cheeked from the cold, holding the end of a trunk of what appeared to be an entire pine tree behind him. Behind that, the smaller of the two Ancestral Fires burned. It burned for every ancestor who had fought for this land, for every wolf who had ever called this place home and given their life to protect it. We lit the bonfire at the start of December, just like every Pack did each year, and it would continue to burn through the entire month.

The biggest Fire was always lit outside the Bottley Bar, but this year, we wanted to have one here, at the Alpha Compound. The walls that had once surrounded this place, keeping the Alphas and enforcers separate from the rest of the Pack, had come down earlier this year. I wanted our Pack to feel comfortable coming here, and I was hoping having an Ancestral Fire here that they could visit all month would help them get used to coming here whenever they wanted.

Ryan blinked at Wally's grinning face. "Why," he asked slowly, "do you have a dead tree?"

"It's not dead, it's festive!" Wally shouldered past Ryan into the house, trailing pine needles across the floor. "And we don't have much time. We have a lot of work to do if we are going to get the whole Three

Rivers decorated!"

Ryan glanced at me. I shrugged at him. I had no idea what Wally was going on about either.

"Decorated for what?"

"Ben's birthday party! Ever since he learned that his birthday fell on the human holiday of Christmas, he's been obsessed with it! Did you know that since their parents died, Amara and Ben have spent the last few years searching for food on his birthday? Can you imagine it?" He waved his hands expressively. "Well, we simply have to do something about that. I sent a call out to everyone I know, then stayed awake all last night researching Christmas."

Ryan pinched the bridge of his nose. "Wally—"

"Now, don't you start with me, Ryan Shaw. Sam's flying in from the Council, and Mason's bringing Shya and Tucker. Thomas is stress-baking enough gingerbread wolves to feed an army, and Derek's picking up decorations."

"Derek knew about this?" Ryan's voice was dangerously low.

"Of course! Someone needed to coordinate all this." Wally planted his hands on his hips. "Now, are you going to help me with this tree or not?"

I couldn't help it—I laughed. The sight of Ryan being steamrolled by our Pack's most determined party planner was too perfect.

Ryan shot me a betrayed look. "You're supporting this?"

I shrugged. "Ben and Amara have been through a lot. He deserves something special. We all do. This might be just what the Pack needs to bring everyone together."

"But today? It's our day. Our no-other-people-in-our-vicinity day!"

Wally heaved the tree past Ryan, its branches slapping him gently on the face as they went past. "You can't choose when Christmas is!"

"I'm the Alpha. I'm pretty sure I can," Ryan said, glowering at the tree.

"Fine. Well, you can't choose when Ben's birthday is! Are you really telling me you are going to deprive Ben of the best birthday he has ever had?"

"No, I'm not saying that. I just don't see why the dead tree has to be in my house!"

Wally sighed and shot me a *help-me* look.

"It does smell nice," I said, smiling as Wally struggled to get it upright. "And it might be good to have everyone here, not for business, but for something fun."

I tilted my head to one side and looked at Ryan. He mouthed the words *you owe me sex,* and I grinned at him. I had no problem with that at all.

"Fine." Ryan sighed in defeat and moved to help Wally with the tree.

"Darling, when you see how beautiful this place looks, you'll be thanking me." Wally beamed. "Now, where did I put those lights? And Mai, honey, you might want to hide that chocolate—Thomas is a bundle of nerves wanting to make this birthday good for Ben, and when he gets nervous, he binge eats everything in sight! Why do you think he is making so many cookies?"

"*Thomas* is the nervous one about all this?" Ryan whispered to me. Ever since Amara and Ben had gone to live with Thomas and Wally, they'd both been trying so hard to make their home a safe, welcoming place for the siblings. They loved having Amara and Ben living with them, and I knew both of them would do anything to make Ben's day as special as possible.

"I heard that!"

I caught Ryan's eye across the room and smiled apologetically. Our peaceful couple of days might be ruined, but I had meant it—this was exactly what our Pack needed, a reminder that we weren't just about battles and takeovers, territory and power. We were family.

Even if that family came with an overly enthusiastic party planner who didn't understand the concept of alone time.

Chapter Three

Mai

Eight hours later, Christmas lights twinkled as they lined the fireplace mantle, their soft glow reflecting off the shiny red and silver baubles hanging from the ten-foot tree that dominated the living room. Silver and gold tinsel wound its way around every available surface, and the smell of cinnamon and fresh pine needles filled the air. For a house that, more often than not these days, hosted meetings with our enforcers, along with their heated discussions about territory and defense, it was surprisingly cozy.

Cozy. I never thought I'd say that about the Alpha House. Usually, the place felt suffocating with its history handed down from Oliver, and Jem and Hayley. It was all about secrets and authority and responsibility. But now ... now, it wasn't just home; it actually felt like home.

From where I stood by the window, arms folded across my chest, I watched Ryan and his brothers bicker over the right way to hang mistletoe from the ceiling. Sam, grinning like the mischief-maker he used to be before he joined the Wolf Council, dangled it precariously over Mason's head, lips puckered as if asking for a kiss, while Derek kept trying to flick it out of his hand. Ryan was getting more and more annoyed with all of them, and I was counting the seconds until he snatched it out of Sam's hands and told them to all sit down while he hung it by himself.

I'd been surprised when Sam turned up; I hadn't thought he'd come. He was so busy with the Wolf Council these days and tracking down the witches behind ripple, but he'd mumbled something about needing a break, a distraction, and that he needed to be with family for a few days. I don't know what he was involved in at the Council, but it had bounced the joy right out of him. He was grimmer these days, with a look in his eyes that he had seen things he couldn't unsee. But he'd thrown himself into the celebrations, and it almost felt like we had the old Sam back.

Since he'd been here, the whole Three Rivers had been transformed into a Christmas wonderland, with anywhere that Ben might go covered with tinsel and lights. We'd had to move the inflatable reindeer as all the werewolf pups kept using them for hunting practice and popping them. And I was going to have to wear sunglasses the next time I went to the Bottley Bar; it looked like a tinsel bomb had exploded in there. Wally was definitely of the there-is-no-such-thing-as-too-much-tinsel school of thought.

My eyes shifted to the figure sitting on the plush couch in front of the Christmas tree: Ben, small and still a little too thin, his wide eyes filled with awe, staring at every twinkling light as though the tree was spun from magic. He hadn't stopped staring at the tree since he arrived with Wally and Thomas earlier, eyes shimmering under the soft glow of the lights.

"Is all this really for me?" Ben's voice trembled slightly, still not daring to blink, as if it might all be gone by the time he opened his eyes again.

Wally, picking up Gremlin from the back of the sofa before she could launch herself at the tree, flashed him a grin. "Of course it is, Ben. Every bit of it." He turned and winked at me. "And let me tell you—it wasn't easy getting this lot," he gestured vaguely at the Shaw brothers, "to hang Christmas lights without tangling up every single strand. You would think, given they are two Alphas, a Beta and a Wolf Council member, that they could do it without tangling each other in lights, but no, that proved to be too much for them."

Gremlin glared at Wally. They'd been having a running battle all day, ever since the tree went up, and Gremlin had obviously decided it was the best thing ever to climb. She'd already brought the tree down once before all the decorations went on it, and now Wally was policing the thing like it was the crown jewels, in between helping Sylvie out in the kitchen. It had been Wally's idea to have a family Christmas dinner for Ben's birthday. It was supposed to be a big event where we could give Ben all his presents.

Ben's small mouth grinned wide. The sight made something warm unfurl deep in my chest. Goddess, the kid deserved this. All of it. The gingerbread and orange smell wafting from the table, the snow globes hidden around the house, the stockings full of presents that everyone had brought to give to Ben. I glanced at Wally, who winked at me before giving Ben's hair a playful tousle. Thomas, quieter but no less protective, sat down next to Ben and took a bite out of the gingerbread man he'd swiped from the table.

"Tsk, don't let Sylvie see you with that!" Wally grabbed the cookie from Thomas's hand and stuffed it into his own mouth. "I'm saving you! They're for when everyone is here!"

I smiled. This was it. My family. Pack. It was stronger than blood. These people—Ryan, his brothers, Wally, Thomas, Ben—they weren't just individuals thrown together by circumstance. They were intentional. We were intentional. What we were building here, it was real. It was love and family and protection, all wrapped together like the brightly colored packages under the tree.

My stomach made a loud, unmistakable gurgle. I clutched at it, as if that would be enough to shut it up. Every head in the room turned to me.

Yeah, they didn't need werewolf hearing to know I was hungry.

Ryan was the first to react, his blue eyes narrowing. He turned on his heel in a fluid motion, already halfway across the room toward the kitchen. Sam jumped down from the chair he'd been standing on as Mason pushed Derek back and they both went after Ryan. Thomas shook his head as Wally grinned at me.

"Girl, your little pea has the wolf's appetite down."

Didn't I know it. It felt like every five minutes, I wanted to gnaw my way through big piles of food.

From the kitchen, I could hear the clatter of plates, the sound of drawers opening and closing, and the unmistakable shoo-ing of Sylvie. "Don't you boys mess with that!" she scolded. "I'm making something proper for our Alpha. Don't just go rummagin' through my kitchen like squirrels on caffeine! Out! The lot of you!"

Ryan popped out first, a massive plate of chocolate cake in hand. His face was serious. He was taking my hunger as a personal challenge to feed me up. Next came Sam, who had somehow managed to carry three whole plates filled with an assortment of meats, balancing them precariously on his arms.

Mason followed, holding a platter of what looked like hastily stolen sandwiches. Derek was last, toting the extravagant shrimp cocktail that I'd seen at the back of the fridge this morning, its pink tails sticking oddly out of what seemed like a crystal punch bowl.

"Uh." I blinked, watching the bizarre concoction of food pile up in front of me. Not even the little pea would be able to munch through all of this.

Wally laughed. "You do know Mai's only carrying one baby and not an entire litter, right?"

"Oh, don't discourage them," Thomas said, reaching over and snagging one of the sandwiches as a knock sounded at the front door.

"Shya and Tucker are here!" Ben jumped up. He'd been excited about meeting Tucker all day.

Mason strode to the door and swung it open. Shya stood in the doorway, bundled up in a thick winter coat and her new brushed leather black Prada boots. Mason had bought those for Shya, and she'd spent half an hour on the phone with me last week, gushing about how beautiful they were. Mason yanked Shya to him and kissed her as Tucker burst forward in a blur, his curly hair bouncing against his face. It had been Mason's idea to introduce Tucker and Ben. He wanted Tucker to have some friends outside of their Pack—and how weird was it to think of Mason having his own Pack?—where everyone saw and treated Tucker as one of the Pack princes. Tucker made a bee-line straight toward Ben, whose eyes went wide as Tucker tackled him in a fierce hug.

"You must be Ben! Happy Christmas Birthday!"

Ben blinked. "Uh ... thanks?"

"You okay?" Ryan whispered into my ear as he held up the chocolate cake. He wasn't going to leave me alone until I ate something.

I nodded, taking a bite and trying not to moan. Sylvie was a goddess in the kitchen. "I'm okay. I'm just sorry Jem and Esme aren't here."

Both of them had helped out with decorating the Three Rivers, but neither of them had wanted to come this evening. I hoped Jem's wolf could forgive me someday, that they would both feel at home in our Pack soon, enough that they would come to evenings like these. I felt a pang in my chest at the thought.

"You sure that's all it is? You had another nightmare last night."

Damn it. I'd hoped he hadn't noticed.

I was having nightmares several times a night now, and it was taking its toll. Thomas said it could be part of the pregnancy, with the hormones causing havoc with my subconscious. I knew Ryan was worried, so I was trying to keep as much of it from him as possible. Looks like I was doing a crappy job of it.

Chapter Four

MAI

"I ... it's nothing, really. Stop worrying."

Ryan pressed a soft kiss to my temple. "I'll never stop worrying. You're my everything, Mai. That means my whole world is making sure you're okay and happy."

A warmth spread through my chest, but I still had that pulse of doubt. A familiar, unwelcome visitor lurking at the back of my mind, whispering when I least expected it. I thought I'd done away with that voice long ago, that I'd buried my insecurities after finally becoming Alpha here. I'd proven myself. Time and time again, I had fought, bled, and led. I wasn't the girl running from everything she feared anymore.

But what if I could never really get rid of that doubt? What if it would always be lying in wait for the right moment to rear its head?

I was so scared.

And I hated myself for it.

I'd thought I'd finally exorcised those demons, the ones that whispered I wasn't good enough. I'd thought becoming Alpha had silenced them, but now that I was carrying new life, this time, it wasn't just about me. It wasn't about being capable of leading or fighting anymore; it was about protecting. Not just myself. But our child. And our Pack. Could I really do both?

Images of my nightmares returned—ghastly, vivid, more real than the Christmas tree right in front of me.

I had fought so hard to show everyone I could hold my own, shoulder to shoulder with Ryan and his brothers. But in my dreams, it was always the same. I'd find myself in the middle of a fight, my skin slick with sweat, claws drawn, my body vibrating with the thrill of battle. Ryan would be there, too, fighting back-to-back with me.

But then, something ... something would happen. It was different each time.

A flash to my left. A snarl to my right. And suddenly, I'd falter. Not because I wasn't strong enough—but I hesitated. I hung back. For the first time in my life, I wasn't sure if my baby and I could take the hit. If I could afford the consequences. And in that split second, Ryan would turn—his instincts sharper than mine, protecting me without thinking—but the opening he left would be enough for his opponent to lunge at whoever was fighting beside us.

The faces were always different.

Sometimes, it was Derek, his body crumpling under the weight of his attacker. Sometimes, it was Jase, his maroon wolf lifeless in the snow.

I had dreamed of Sofia once, blood pooling around her hair as I called out her name, but no sound had come from my throat.

Last night, it was Ben.

My nightmares were relentless, as though they were trying to remind me that no matter what I did, my decisions would lead to the death of someone I cared about. And now I constantly wondered, what would happen to our Pack during an attack if I found myself too slow, too distracted by my fear for our child? I had always trusted my instincts in battle. Now, I wasn't so sure.

I couldn't afford to be vulnerable.

I felt Ryan's eyes on me. Ryan. Steady and watchful, sensing, as always, something shifting within me.

I had to figure this out. I had to find a way to silence that voice inside that said I wasn't strong enough to do it all.

Because the alternative was too terrible to imagine. I wouldn't let anyone be harmed because of me. Not our baby. Not Derek. Not Jase. Not Sofia. Not Ben.

Not Ryan.

Fuck! I didn't know how to deal with this. Ryan was right. I was on edge; I was letting my temper flare up, but it was like I had no control over it. One minute, I was calm, the next, I wanted to rip out the throat of the next person who breathed within a ten-foot radius around me. What if I lost my temper during a fight? If I made rash decisions in the heat of battle rather than being clear-headed and calculating? What if I made a mistake, put me and the baby at risk, and forced Ryan to come and protect us, leaving someone else vulnerable?

I had to tell Ryan. He knew me too well. He'd seen the nightmares wear at me, pick at the edges of my sanity in the dead of night. He'd kissed away the sweat on my forehead in the mornings, held me tighter in ways that made everything feel alright for just a moment. But that wouldn't last. Not if I didn't deal with this head-on.

I swallowed.

"Mai?"

Right. Of course, he could feel what I was feeling through our bond.

He shook his head and growled. "This is why I wanted it to be just us tonight. We need to talk. Properly. Without the rest of the Pack around. I'm going to get to the bottom of what's in your head, Mai, and we're going to sort it out."

"Rya—"

"I told you to stop doing that!" Amara stomped into the room, her blue hair a wild mess from the winter wind. Cameron Blake, one of our enforcers who had just started dating Amara, followed her in.

"Doing what? Being nice?" Cameron's voice was calm, though I caught the slight upturn at the corner of his mouth. "Because that's all I did. I bought you a coffee."

"It wasn't just a coffee!" Amara spun around, jabbing a finger at his chest. "It was some fancy caramel-praline-whatever thing with extra whipped cream and those little chocolate sprinkles I mentioned liking ONE TIME three weeks ago!"

Ben eyed Cameron warily, clearly not yet sure whether to take his sister's side or not.

"Oh, I'm sorry," Cameron drawled, crossing his arms. "I didn't realize remembering what you like was a capital offense."

"That's not—" Amara spluttered, her cheeks flushing. "You can't just—people don't just do things like that!"

"Normal people do," Wally chimed in helpfully. "It's called being thoughtful, honey."

Amara shot him a glare that could have melted steel. "Stay out of this!"

I felt Ryan's chest rumble with silent laughter against my back.

"And the scarf!" She yanked at the soft-looking green fabric around her neck. "I didn't ask for this!"

"You were shivering," Cameron stated matter-of-factly. "It's winter. People wear scarves in winter."

"I can buy my own scarves!"

"Of course you can. But I saw this one and thought of you. That's allowed, you know. Boyfriends do that sometimes."

The word "boyfriends" seemed to throw Amara even more off-balance. She opened and closed her mouth several times, clearly searching for another argument and coming up empty.

Finally, she threw her hands up in defeat. "You're impossible!" She stomped over to where Ben sat, flopping down next to him with a dramatic huff, though I noticed she didn't take the scarf off.

Ryan, with his annoying habit of never forgetting anything, looked at me. "You were going to say something."

I exhaled slowly and nodded. "Later. Right now, let's just enjoy this."

He didn't argue with me, which told me he knew just how important this moment felt. The balance of it all—the warmth, the safety—was too fragile to disturb right then. But his arm slipped around my waist, pulling me to his side, and for a heartbeat, I let myself lean into him, just feeling his steady presence.

"You know I'm here, right? No matter what? We'll figure it out."

We'll figure it out.

I closed my eyes and let his words wash over me, allowing myself to believe it, even if just for tonight.

Chapter Five

SOFIA

I sat in the quiet of my car, the hum of the engine the only thing tethering me to reality as the December air pressed in from all sides, turning the windows foggy. It had been ... what, ten minutes now? Ten ridiculously long minutes, and I still hadn't stepped out. My fingers gripped the steering wheel tighter, cramping, but I couldn't seem to get them to relax.

"Come on, Sofia," I muttered under my breath. "You've done scarier things than this. It's just a house. With people in it that you actually like."

For the Goddess's sake! I ran the Bottley Bar and Coffee Shop, I managed a team of eight, dealt with angry customers, drunk werewolves, and humans who were too touchy for their own good on a daily basis. Now, here I was, parked outside a family party, acting like an awkward teenager at a prom. Because of him.

Damn it, Derek.

I hated the reaction my body had to even thinking his name. The sudden jolt in my pulse, the heat that curled low in my stomach. He had no right to make me feel like this—undone and out of control—and yet here I was. Derek Shaw, the infuriating enigma that he was, had slithered beneath my skin and taken root there, and no matter what I did, I couldn't get rid of him.

I should just go home. Forget about all this, go back to my apartment, crack open a bottle of wine, and watch a holiday rom-com. Derek didn't deserve a second of my time—but more than that, I didn't deserve to turn into the confusing puddle of a mess every damn time he entered the same room as me.

No. I was not going to let him chase me off. Me, Sofia Miller. The woman who'd fought alongside the best of our Pack in defeating Brock and hadn't flinched once.

No. Hell, no. I wasn't running just because of Derek fucking Shaw.

I breathed deep, turned off the engine, and grabbed my bag from the passenger seat.

As soon as I stepped out, the cold hit me, and I put a smile on my face—the cool air grounding me in a way I couldn't. I was here for Ben and for my Pack. My family. I just needed to remember that.

I glanced up at the Alpha House, its massive outline softened by twinkling Christmas lights strung along the roof. The windows glowed with soft, golden light, warmth seeping out like a promise. It was beautiful, inviting—and for a moment, I let myself feel comforted by the idea that inside, there was laughter, joy, and probably a ridiculous amount of food, if Sylvie and Wally had anything to do with it. This wasn't about Derek. It was about spending time with the people I cared about and making some damned good memories that had nothing to do with Pack battles or missions gone wrong.

Pulling my jacket tighter around myself, I squared my shoulders and put on my game face—the one I had perfected over years of smiling through the pain of my parents leaving, my best friend Mai leaving, Derek fucking Shaw up and joining the military, coming back to woo the pants off me, literally, and then ghosting me for months.

No, I was confident. Unshakable. I was Sofia Miller, barista extraordinaire, who welcomed everyone into the Bottley and made sure they felt like we were their family. I wasn't going to let anyone see how lonely I really felt.

I could do this. Really, I could.

I pushed through the door and was immediately hit in the face by a flying cushion.

"What the f—?"

"Language, Sofia!" Wally appeared and took the cushion from me. "Sorry, darling! I was aiming for that devil cat!"

"Gremlin?"

"No, Gremlin is sweetness personified. She is adorable. I can only conclude this is Gremlin's evil twin, who is hell-bent on bringing the whole tree down so she can spend the evening batting all the baubles around the house."

I glanced into the living room to see a Christmas tree sparkling in the corner. Gremlin was sitting by the sofa, nonchalantly licking her paw.

I looked back at the front door. "Wally, she is nowhere near the door."

"You know his aim is terrible!" Thomas said as he kissed my cheek.

"Sofia! Get in here!" Mai shouted.

I walked into the living room to see Mai smiling at me with her arm around Ryan's waist. It suited her—this role as the Alpha, and now the freaking pregnant Alpha. I couldn't wait to meet the little pup.

Without a doubt, I would make sure I was their favorite aunt.

This was why I had come. Mai, Wally, Thomas ... they were my family. They were the reason I was here, despite everything rattling around in my chest, despite the constant storm that brewed whenever a certain someone decided to stroll into the room.

And speak of the devil.

I casually glanced toward the far end of the living room, and sure enough, there he was, leaning against the wall, wearing a fitted black shirt that did absolutely nothing to diminish the strong, lean lines of his body. Of course, he looked ridiculously good, despite the tension I could see pulling at the hard lines of his jaw. His arms were crossed over his chest, and those cool gray eyes were already locked onto me. His scent hit me like a hot splash of water—pine and moss, unmistakable even with the scent of mulled cider floating through the room. And then there was that feeling—that distinct awareness coursing through me whenever he was in the same room, like every nerve had been rewired specifically to know when he was near. It was ridiculous how my body responded to him. The temperature could have dropped twenty degrees, and I still would have heated up at just the sight of him.

For fuck's sake! It was like this every damn time. It made me want to throw a cushion at *his* head. A solid, soul-satisfying toss right between the eyes.

My wolf perked up at the sight of him. She had no doubts about who her mate was and thought I was being ridiculous for not jumping him wherever he was in range.

"Earth to Sofia," Wally said in a sing-song tone, pulling me back to the present. He nudged my side with his elbow, giving me a knowing look. "You okay? You look like you just swallowed a particularly spicy candy cane. And I don't mean the pepper kind."

I forced my eyes away from Derek, though every cell in my body screamed in protest. "Just wondering if Ben is going to like the present I got him."

"Deflection!" Wally waggled his finger at me. "That's deflection, honey, and we both know it. You haven't taken your eyes off our resident brooding wolf since you walked in. Well, except for right now, when you're very deliberately not looking at him."

"I don't know what you're talking about," I said, straightening my sweater with far more attention than it needed.

"Oh, honey, the sexual tension between you two is so thick I could frost a cake with it. And trust me, I know my frostings."

Oh, wonderful. Of course Wally had noticed.

I put on my best I-don't-have-a-care-in-the-world smile and waved my hand airily. "I don't know what you're talking about! I'm just here to celebrate the best birthday party the Three Rivers can put on. Where is the birthday boy, anyway?"

"Girl, you might get away with that at work, but you can't fool me. Besides, Derek is over there not only looking like he wants to devour you but that, in his mind, he is doing precisely that."

I swallowed; that image in *my* mind was making my panties wet.

"Wally," I warned, "now is not the time."

"Sofia," he mimicked back, "it is never the time with you. I want to know what is going on! I thrive on gossip! You and Derek are a hot cake of the good stuff, but you never tell me anything anymore! I need my daily dose, girl!"

He looked at me with pleading eyes.

"Fine," I said through gritted teeth. "But not today. We'll do a girls' night with Mai and Shya, alright?"

His grin widened, "I knew you wouldn't let me down!"

I knew Derek was watching. Always watching. He had this irritating talent for being able to sense when I was frazzled, or worse, pretending I wasn't frazzled.

I plastered a smile on my face and focused on the swirl of whipped cream in my mug, the sound of Sam and Mason bickering in the background, and the gentle hum of holiday music drifting from the speakers Ryan had installed around the house. Anything but the constant pull in my gut that told me, over and over again, that Derek Shaw was standing just over there, watching me.

I heard the footsteps first, the soft click of his boots across the hardwood floor. And then, without even needing to turn around, I knew he was near. Not right beside me, but close enough to make the back of my neck tingle, to make my wolf rise to meet the challenge of our proximity.

"Sofia," his voice drawled low and controlled, the way it always did when he was about to say something infuriating.

"Not tonight, Derek."

He leaned casually against the edge of the table. "Not even hello? And here I was thinking you missed me."

"I don't want to play your games, Derek."

"I'm not playing, Sofia."

I snapped my gaze to his face, ready to lay out all the games he'd played in the past—but instead, I froze, my breath catching in my throat. His gray eyes locked onto mine with an intensity that made the air between us feel like it was going to combust.

I was damn tired of how easily he could do this to me. Goddess, it had to stop.

He leaned down, his lips next to my ear as he whispered, "I mean it. I'm not playing."

It took a herculean effort for me to step back. "You're about as subtle as a gnat trying to land a bite, Derek. All this," I waved my hand up and down, "being broody and sexy. It has no effect on me whatsoever," I lied.

He lifted a brow, the smirk on his face making me want to kick him. "Broody and sexy?"

I narrowed my eyes at him. "No. Effect. Whatsoever."

I made a move to flounce away—I'd always been good at flouncing and had used it to good effect as a teenager. I needed to put space between us, but his hand shot out and gently grasped my arm. It wasn't forceful, but it sent a jolt of energy through me, as though he'd just injected me with pure adrenaline.

"Sofia," he said softly, but there was something firm, something pressing behind his words. Oh, no. Not this again. Not the soft, vulnerable voice, not the way he said my name like it was some kind of sacred chant. It was always like this—Derek being a fortress of steel until, suddenly, he wasn't. And each time he'd crack, each time he'd say something that made me believe—just for a moment—that I was important to him, it only made me angrier when the walls slammed back up.

I didn't want to be important. When I got involved with someone,

I wanted to be everything.

"Just—" I sighed, voice cracking in frustration. "What do you want, Derek? Besides tormenting me."

A shadow crossed his face. "I don't want to torment you." His tone was too raw, too honest. The kind of honesty that threatened to dismantle every defense I'd built around myself. "But I can't—"

"—can't stay away and can't stick around either?"

His fingers flexed around my arm, not gripping harder, just ... holding me steady, as though even his body was begging me not to misunderstand.

"It's complicated."

"Yeah? Well, you're a hot-shot military intelligence guru. Make it uncomplicated. Then we'll talk."

With that, I yanked my arm out of his hand and performed a flounce that my teenage self would have been proud of.

Chapter Six

RYAN

I could feel Mai's eyes from across the room, and I tried to school my face into something more neutral. Easier said than done. Part of me was overjoyed to see her laughing at something Shya had just said, her eyes momentarily lighting up with something close to peace as she glanced at me. It had been far too long since I'd seen that look on her. Too long since I hadn't felt her tiredness, her fear. Our mate bond hummed with humor, but there was still something else beneath it—an undercurrent of fear, anxiety, a sharp edge that she couldn't seem to push down.

She caught my eye and lifted one brow in that way she did whenever she knew I was trying to figure her out. I gave her a little nod—a silent "I'm watching you." She flashed a small grin in return, but it didn't quiet the tension inside me.

I wished I could solve whatever was bothering her. But whatever it was—this fear that had wormed its way into her thoughts and dreams—it wasn't something my fists or claws could fix. This wasn't a fight. It was something else. Something deeper. Instinctively, I felt my wolf shift under my skin, restless and growling, demanding I do something to make it right. But until I knew what was going on inside of her head, I had no idea what to do. My fists clenched. This wasn't an enemy I could kill, and it was driving me and my wolf nuts. Was it about the baby? I was trying to be strong for Mai, but I was scared shitless about what dangers our kids would have to face in this world. We were Alphas, and that meant we had a target on our backs at all times. Could I protect them both? They just had to get it right once to kill one of us. I would have to get it right every fucking time to protect my family.

My phone rang in my pocket, and I glanced down at the screen.

Jase's name flashed across the display.

I hit the connect button. "Yeah?"

"Ryan, there's a guy at the western perimeter. Says his name is Maxwell Bishop."

Maxwell Bishop? I cursed under my breath. *Bishop.* As in, Ronnie Bishop. The last thing I needed right now was some complication involving Ronnie's mess of biker affairs.

"As in—?"

"Yeah, he says he's Ronnie's brother."

Just fucking great.

"What the hell does he want?"

"He's got a werewolf pup with him, Ryan. A girl about ten years old. Looks terrified as hell. Says they need help."

My gaze instinctively scanned the room, finding Mai. Her eyes met mine, and even across the room, I could feel her wolf rising. She sensed it. Something was wrong.

Fuck. I wanted tonight to be special for Mai. Family, food, relaxing times, not some mess the Bishops had dumped in our laps. But we needed to know what the hell he wanted before I sent them on their way.

"Bring them here. Make sure they're not tailed."

"You got it." Jase ended the call, and I tucked the phone back into my pocket just as Mai got to me, a question on her face.

I sighed. "Jase is bringing Maxwell Bishop, Ronnie's brother, and a young werewolf girl here. They're at the western perimeter, asking for help."

"Help? What sort of help?"

"That's what we're gonna find out. It shouldn't take long. We'll be done before dinner's ready."

I hoped that was true. Mai needed this meal with all of us together. We all did.

"Alright," she murmured as she tipped her chin up slightly. "But if Maxwell is here, where the hell is Ronnie?"

"That's the first question I'm going to ask him."

Fifteen minutes later, I stood in the brisk air just outside the Alpha House, the twinkling light streaming from around the windows behind me onto the frost-covered front yard. Even the yard and the cul-de-sac hadn't escaped Wally's decorations. The whole place looked like a damn Christmas card had exploded all over it—complete with an army of light-up reindeer, a massive inflatable snowman that swayed eerily in the winter breeze, and enough strands of twinkling lights to probably be visible from space. Wally had even managed to convince Derek and Sam to string lights through all the trees lining the street, creating a glowing tunnel effect that was admittedly pretty impressive, even if it had taken them three hours and a lot of cursing to get it done.

I heard the crunch of the car approaching. Then a black SUV pulled up and Jase got out, his face full of wariness. From the passenger seat, a man appeared. Tall, definitely over six feet, with a broad chest and lean, muscular arms. His movements were sharp, deliberate. But what struck me more than his physique was the gleam in his sharp, assessing eyes. Not the kind of man who missed much.

Maxwell Bishop. He was Ronnie's brother, alright. I could see it in the bone structure—strong jaw, sharp cheekbones, the same intense stare Ronnie had, though Maxwell's felt ... colder. More clinical. Where Ronnie exuded rebellion, chaos, and a near carelessness, Maxwell felt like precision personified. There were no unnecessary movements with him. His presence radiated control.

A slight figure jumped out of the car behind Maxwell, one small hand clutching his jacket and half-hiding behind his legs. The scent hit me before I had a clear look at her—a young werewolf, frightened but strong. Her hair was dark brown, practically black, thick and wild around her small, pale face. It fell in jagged, uneven lengths, as if someone had tried cutting it with a blade and, somewhere along the way, gave up. Despite the way it hid most of her features, her eyes still peeked out from under her bangs, watching me warily.

Then the girl, small and fragile as she appeared, shifted her stance, almost as if on instinct. That brief flicker of motion, that loosening of her small hands around the hem of his jacket, was enough to set every nerve in my body alight with recognition.

It wasn't that she was hiding behind him out of fear. No, this wasn't an instinct to shield herself. She was positioning herself to protect him.

Interesting.

The movement was small, not even noticeable to Maxwell, whose eyes were scanning the compound like he was mapping every exit.

"Ryan," Jase greeted me with a quick nod, his eyes flicking between me and Maxwell. "No one followed. Just these two."

Maxwell raised both hands, palms out, in a pacifying gesture as he neared the steps, but his blue eyes remained sharp, assessing the threat.

I met Maxwell's eyes briefly as he stepped closer, but he instinctively broke contact, looking down and keeping his posture low—a subtle show of submission. The guy knew what he was doing. He clearly had experience around wolves. He knew not to challenge my dominance, not even a little.

My wolf stirred under my skin, curious, cautious.

Maxwell kept his movements slow and precise. "Ryan Shaw."

I crossed my arms. "You show up out of nowhere, at the edge of my territory, with someone else's pup. I hope you've got a damn good reason."

"I do." He nodded to the girl. "Her Pack is hunting her. I want you to protect her."

Chapter Seven

Mai

I watched Ryan come in the front door, followed by Jase and the man who must be Maxwell Bishop. His eyes flickered briefly toward me, then Sam, Derek, and Mason, calculating quickly, taking note of his surroundings like a seasoned soldier entering enemy territory. My focus shifted quickly from him to the small figure by his side—a girl; couldn't be more than ten or eleven. Her fingers clutched the bottom of Maxwell's jacket, knuckles white from the pressure, though she stood off from him, ready to move if needed. Her dark eyes darted between us, wide and alert, like a wolf just released into a new stretch of wilderness. She was lean, slightly underfed by the look of it, with a nose that was a smidge too large for her face. She came to a stop, angling her body between Maxwell and the rest of us.

Pack instincts.

She had them. Whether she was conscious of them or not. And she wanted to protect the human.

Then, her eyes landed on the gigantic Christmas tree. She took it all in with wide, unblinking eyes, her wariness shifting momentarily into something else entirely. Awe.

Ryan stepped toward me, his hand brushing the small of my back for only a second, but it was enough to ground me.

"Hello. I'm Mai."

The man nodded at me, keeping his eyes on my chin. "Maxwell. Maxwell Bishop."

Ryan wasted no time getting to the point. "Where's Ronnie?"

The corners of Maxwell's mouth briefly tightened, but he didn't flinch. "He's handling a situation out east."

Right.

"I don't suppose you're here carol-singing?"

A smile flickered across Maxwell's face. "No, I'm not much of a singer."

"Right," I sighed. It had been too much to hope for. "Well then, we should take this to the study."

Ryan sent a glance toward his brothers, telling them to come with us. Out of the corner of my eye, I saw Jase glaring at Amara and Cameron. Yeah, he was not happy she was dating someone. And that it was Cameron, the boy-scout enforcer who everyone loved? That only made it worse. Jase had been grumpy as hell since they'd gotten together.

I turned as Sylvie appeared from the kitchen with the same brisk efficiency she always carried. Today, she wore her short, chestnut-brown hair in a sharp, clean cut that framed her face with effortless style—a practical look that suited her straightforward nature. There was no pretension in the way she looked or moved. Even her clothes hinted at functional simplicity: dark blue jeans and a loose blouse. Three purple stud earrings glinted in each ear beneath her tousled hair. Sylvie took one look at all the people here, her face paled, and she made a sharp U-turn. She avoided crowds, refusing to go to Pack events or even eat with us. She was the best cook this side of the Whispering Willow, but she'd spent too much time alone before coming here to be comfortable with many people, even members of her own Pack.

I caught Maxwell staring after her. His eyes flickered with something—a flash of recognition or surprise. Interesting. Did he know Sylvie?

Something to ask her later.

"Ben," I called, keeping my tone gentle. "Come here a second."

Ben, who had been watching everything from his spot by the fireplace, stepped forward cautiously.

"Can you show—uh ..." I turned to the girl. "What's your name, sweetheart?"

The girl's lips parted, but for a second, nothing came out. She dropped her head a little, staring down at the tips of her shoes. "... Lark."

Her eyes flicked up to meet mine for a brief, fleeting moment, then quickly shifted back down to the floor.

"I was wondering, Lark," I began gently, "if you might like to check out the house? Ben and his friend Tucker here could show you around. We have a big tree, lots of snacks, and maybe—if Thomas hasn't eaten them all yet—some cookies."

"Yeah, we could show you all the best places," Ben said shyly. "There's even a room with lots of books and cool secret spaces."

Tucker, bouncing on the toes of his feet, nudged in front of Ben. "Come on, we can show you the kitchen too! That's where the gingerbread wolves are and where Mason pretends he doesn't pinch them." He grinned mischievously, clearly proud of his knowledge.

Shya laughed as Ben said urgently, "I told you to keep that a secret!"

"Don't worry, Ben, that's not a secret—everyone knows Mason can't resist a gingerbread wolf when he sees one."

Lark hesitated, her small frame remaining stiff by Maxwell's side. He leaned down toward her, murmuring, "Go on. I'll be right here, Lark."

Her grip on his jacket finally released. She took a small, tentative step toward Ben and Tucker. They grinned at her as she followed them deeper into the house. I nodded to Jase, and he followed them.

Ryan didn't waste any more time. He turned sharply toward Maxwell and jerked his head toward the door leading to the study. Maxwell stepped forward, glancing only once in the direction Lark had gone before following Ryan. I trailed after them, Mason, Derek, and Sam all falling into step behind us.

By the time Maxwell, Ryan, and I had sat down, with Mason leaning against the desk, Derek propping up the far wall where he could keep an eye on everyone in the room, and Sam perching on the edge of one of the leather couches, looking relaxed to anyone who didn't know him, Ryan was clearly losing patience. "Alright, Maxwell, you've got five minutes to explain what the hell's going on."

Maxwell nodded once. "I don't have all the answers, but what I know is this: Ronnie found Lark about two months ago. She had run away from her Pack and was terrified about something that had happened there. He took her in and made sure she was kept safe. For a while. But ..." He paused. His eyes flicked to the side momentarily, as if calculating whether or not to share more.

"But?" I prompted.

Maxwell exhaled slowly, choosing his next words carefully. "Ronnie called me two days ago. We're ... well, we're not close. Not these days. I live down south now and don't hear much from my brother."

"What did he say?"

"Ronnie needed a favor, said it was something only I could do. Didn't tell me what, just said to get to the clubhouse asap. We might not be close anymore, but I owe Ronnie. I got on a plane first thing. I got to the clubhouse yesterday and ... well, Lark was there with two prospects, along with a handwritten note from Ronnie that said, 'Protect the girl, trust no one.'"

Movement outside the frosted window caught my eye. The three children were outside, Jase hovering in the distance. Tucker threw a snowball at Ben, laughing and spinning in pure delight. Lark was standing a few feet away from the boys, watching them as though deciding if it was worth joining in.

"You said her Pack wants her back." Ryan's deep voice drew me back inside the study. "Do you know which Pack she's from?"

Maxwell shook his head, grimacing slightly. "That's where I'm in the dark. I've asked Lark, but she's not talking. All I got out of her was that her parents are dead, and she doesn't ever want to go back to her Pack. According to the prospects, Ronnie is determined to keep her, and the whole fucking club has been acting as her family for the last two months; even been home-schooling her."

"No Pack is going to let a pup make a decision like that," Sam pointed out.

"So I gather. Apparently, they turned up last week and demanded Ronnie return her. He refused. They left, but then four days ago, Benny—he's a patch holder, someone Ronnie trusts—stumbled into the shop, covered in blood, saying there was an attack on Ronnie's operations across the north."

"The Pack is taking down his businesses until he relents," I guessed.

"Yeah. Only if you know anything about Ronnie, you know he doesn't relent. He left to take care of them. He couldn't take the girl with him, not if he wanted to keep her safe—"

"So he called the one person he trusts to protect her," said Sam.

Maxwell nodded.

Mason, still leaning against the desk, crossed one ankle over the other. "Yet you brought her here?"

"Ronnie finally fucking picked up my call last night. He told me that if things got too hot, to bring the girl here. Then he hung up on me."

Maxwell was clearly as unhappy about this whole situation as we were.

"And it got too hot?" Derek asked.

Maxwell's jaw was tight, and he was silent for a moment before answering. "They came this morning. Before dawn. Ten werewolves. They torched the clubhouse. Killed one of the prospects. I got away with Lark. Sent the other prospect to find Ronnie."

Sam smiled a smile that didn't reach his eyes. "That's pretty darn impressive, man. One human escaping from ten werewolves."

Maxwell leveled his gaze at Sam, and there was a dangerous glint in his eyes. He was just as lethal as his brother, and we'd be fools to underestimate him. "I'm a Bishop. We're never helpless, not even against Shifters. But I can't protect her by myself, and I've got no fucking clue when Ronnie will be back." Then he leaned back against the couch. "So, will you help us?"

CHAPTER EIGHT

SYLVIE

I smelled him first, then thought I was imagining it. It wouldn't be the first time I'd thought I'd scented him. Over the last few years, I'd thought I'd caught his scent more than once. Each time, my heart fluttered, my palms got sweaty, and I'd try to track down where the smell was coming from. Each time, it had all been in my imagination. So, I think I can be forgiven for thinking it would be the same today.

Except it wasn't the same. The moment I saw him, I knew. He was really here. Even after all these years, Maxwell Bishop still carried himself with that same quiet intensity, that careful control that masked the predator beneath. He was older now, lines at the corners of his eyes that hadn't been there before, but everything else—the broad shoulders, the tattoos that snaked up his arms, the way he assessed a room, the small crook in his nose from an old break—was exactly as I remembered.

I'd taken one look, turned on my heel, and headed straight back to the kitchen, trying not to hyperventilate. I busied myself with the pot of mulled wine simmering on the stove, ignoring the way my hands trembled as I added another cinnamon stick. I needed to make hot chocolate for the kids. They would like that. The kitchen was my sanctuary, had been ever since Jem took me in two years ago. Here, I paid my penance for what I did; I could hide from the crowds, from the noise, from everything that reminded me of my old life. But now that life had walked right through the shitting front door.

And with it, memories of a different December. Of Grace, my older sister, before everything went wrong, baking in our tiny apartment kitchen. She would hum off-key while measuring ingredients, flour in her hair, telling me about our future bakery.

"We'll call it Sisters' Sweet Spot. And we'll never have to answer to anyone but ourselves."

But then she met Levi, a member of the local werewolf biker gang, and suddenly, her dreams of opening a bakery became dreams of quick money and power. The sister who'd taught me to bake snickerdoodles became someone who taught me to case buildings and run lookout.

"This is our family now," she'd said. "Pack. This is where we belong." But it hadn't felt like belonging. It had felt like drowning.

Then Maxwell had walked into that dingy bar on the outskirts of some run-down town. Maxwell's hands, rough but gentle, as he'd pulled me close ...

No! I couldn't think about that now.

The cocoa powder slipped from my trembling fingers, spilling across the counter. "Shit."

"Here, let me help."

Wally's cheerful voice made me jump. He swept in like a whirlwind, already reaching for a cloth. "Though I have to say, if you're going to have a kitchen crisis, cocoa powder is definitely the prettiest mess to clean up. Much better than that time Jase tried to make homemade fish sauce."

I managed a weak smile, grateful for his help but wishing my hands would stop shaking as I tried to clean up.

"You know," Wally said casually—too casually—as he wiped down the counter, "I couldn't help but notice that little gasp when you saw our mysterious visitor. I know a wow-that-is-one-hot-guy reaction when I see it."

If he only knew.

"Wally—"

"Plus," he continued, "you're making hot chocolate, and I know baking is your go-to stress-busting activity. Though technically, it's called stress-baristaing, I suppose? "

I sighed. "I'm fine. Really."

"Mmhmm." Wally raised an eyebrow, clearly not buying it. "You know, just because you hide yourself away in this kitchen doesn't mean we don't see you, sweetie. And not just because you make the best damn snickerdoodles this side of the Mississippi."

"I'm not hiding."

I was so hiding. I had spent years trying to make myself forgettable, to blend into the background. It was safer that way. Easier. After everything that happened with Grace's gang, I deserved to fade away, didn't I? To be nothing more than a quiet shadow.

"Oh, please." He put his hands on his hips. "You're more ghost than housekeeper sometimes. But here's the thing—you're part of this Pack, and we love you."

Something in my chest tightened. This Pack meant everything to me. They'd saved me when I had no one else. Jem had taken me in, given me a job, allowed me to heal, to hide because that was exactly what I needed.

But sometimes … sometimes I missed the old Sylvie. The one who used to dance in thunderstorms and race motorcycles under the full moon. The one who wasn't afraid to take up space, to be wild and free and spontaneous. The one who'd spent a mind-blowing night with Maxwell Bishop.

"Earth to Sylvie!" Wally waved a hand in front of my face. "You're doing that thing again where you disappear into your head. Though," he grinned wickedly, "given the way that man in there fills out his jeans, I can't say I blame you."

"Wally!" I felt my cheeks flush.

"What? I'm married, not blind." He bumped his hip against mine playfully. "And Thomas agrees with me, by the way. We will be discussing Mr. Tall-Dark-and-Brooding's assets later, and let me tell you—"

"Oh, my Goddess, stop!" But I was laughing now, really laughing.

"There she is," Wally said softly, his smile gentle. "You know, that laugh of yours is too pretty to keep locked away in here all the time." Then his eyes sparkled with mischief. "Though if you're determined to stay in the kitchen, might I suggest the pantry? It's quite roomy, and I happen to know it locks from the inside …"

"Wally!" I swatted at him with the dish towel, my face burning.

He ducked, cackling. "Just saying! A girl's got needs, and that man looks like he could fulfill quite a few of them."

Oh, I knew he could. But that, that was the old Sylvie. Not who I was now.

"So," he said, diving into the pantry to grab the bag of marshmallows from their hiding spot, "let's make these kids the best damn hot chocolate they've ever had. And if a certain someone happens to want a cup, too ..." He waggled his eyebrows suggestively.

If Maxwell wanted a cup of hot chocolate, I'd make sure Wally was the one who handed it out.

Chapter Nine

Mai

Ryan's jaw was clenched tight. I knew he was considering Maxwell's request for help, but he was pissed off about it. He wasn't wrong to be angry. We were already juggling enough with integrating the rogue wolves left over from Korrin's attacks into our Pack, the ripple crisis, and trying to find the witches involved in it. And now, we had a werewolf child in our house whose very presence could bring a shitstorm down on us.

I had questions—so many questions—and not enough answers. I wasn't sure that Maxwell knew anything else though.

I stood and walked to the door. I cracked the door open and called out for Sylvie. She arrived smelling of cocoa powder and cinnamon. Her eyes darted around the room, hesitating a moment too long on Maxwell.

"Sylvie," I said. "Could you take Maxwell to the kitchen and get him something to eat, please?"

Her scent turned wary. Was this her usual reluctance to be with others or something else?

"Sylvie? I can ask someone else?" I kept my tone gentle, giving her a way out if she wanted one.

Her face turned determined. "It's no bother. Maxwell, is it?"

He stared at her for a moment longer before answering. "Yes. Maxwell."

Sylvie nodded. "Okay, then. Follow me."

Maxwell hesitated for just a second, tossed a glance back at Ryan and me, then followed Sylvie out of the room.

I watched the study door close behind them. Ryan rubbed a hand slowly down his face and exhaled; the weariness and frustration in that sound sharpened my awareness of how annoyed he was that Ronnie had put us in this position.

Maxwell Bishop and a frightened werewolf girl on the run from an unknown Pack that wanted her back. There were many issues with this, but the main problem was we still didn't know if we were on the right side of it.

"Thoughts?" I asked.

"It's one thing to help a stray werewolf pup," Ryan replied. "It's another to take on the very real possibility of her Pack coming after her. Coming after us. And I gotta say, if it was one of our pups, I'd burn the fucking world down getting them back. We don't know why Lark left or what happened with her Pack. We can't even be sure Maxwell's story is right. Even if he is telling the truth, he heard it from Ronnie's prospects. Who knows what the situation actually is."

"Ronnie Bishop has some fucking nerve," Derek muttered from his spot by the door. "Dumping a kid at our doorstep like this. What the hell is that guy thinking?"

Sam ran a hand through his hair. "I'm betting he's thinking he has few options left."

"Yeah?" Mason snorted. "He knew he screwed up, so he goes and tosses the bomb in our lap, hoping we can clean up his mess."

Derek shook his head slowly. "She's just a kid. A scared kid. But taking her in—it puts everyone in the Three Rivers at risk. The whole Pack. We don't know what we're facing. We don't have a clue who this other Pack is and what their resources are. Would it be worth it?"

I could feel everyone in the room shifting on the edge of that line. Were we prepared to handle more enemies right now? Could we risk the fragile peace we were trying to build?

I let my eyes flick toward the window, watching the hints of snowflakes gently swirling in through the light of the house before landing on a patch of untouched white outside. In the distance, Lark stood, hesitating at the edge of where Ben and Tucker were throwing snowballs, trying to convince her to join in.

She looked so small compared to the two boys. Fragile but sharp. She was on alert. Not relaxed the way kids should be—hell, the way most of our Pack pups were when they felt safe. She wasn't safe yet. Even here, she knew she was in danger.

"I didn't know Ronnie had a brother," I glanced at Ryan. "Did you?'

"You wouldn't," Derek cut in before Ryan could reply. Derek was our Beta, but he'd worked in the military as an intelligence officer, and when he came out, he'd wanted to use his skills to make the Three Rivers Pack secure. Recently, he'd found out that there were people from his past who were targeting Sofia because of her connection to him. He was on edge all the time. He wasn't going to let anyone harm Sofia, but with her still wanting nothing to do with him, she wasn't making protecting her easy. So, it didn't surprise me that Derek had thoroughly investigated anyone connected to us, and that meant the Bishops.

"Maxwell isn't easy to find. Not many people outside the gang know about him ... well, most wouldn't even peg him as Ronnie's brother. He split from their gang a while back, went legit, and now works down south, according to my sources. But before that, he was right in the middle of all of it. Ronnie and Maxwell were groomed to run the Bishop gang together. If things hadn't changed? He'd probably still be out there, right beside Ronnie."

"So, what happened?"

"We don't know. Something big enough to make Maxwell give everything up, move across the country, and become a lawyer. He walked away from everything their family stood for."

Frustration flickered across Ryan's face, his hand kneading the back of his neck as if trying to get all those warring instincts to quiet. "Look, we don't owe Ronnie anything. We aren't exactly on good terms. So, if we're going to take a stand defending this girl, we'd better be ready for whatever crosses our doorstep. And that means understanding if Ronnie's really protecting her or if she's somehow an asset for him to leverage, and he's actually keeping a pup from her Pack."

The silence that followed was broken by the muffled laughter coming from outside the window—the soft sounds of Ben and Tucker playing their game of snowballs. Lark still stood on the edge, watching them with a look of yearning on her face. In that moment, I knew she desperately wanted to join in but didn't know how. What the hell kind of Pack had she come from? My chest tightened. Hell, she was a kid—just a kid who had been through more than she should have.

Mason leaned against the desk, considering Ryan's words carefully. "You think we should give her back?" His words didn't carry judgment, but they shook something loose inside me.

Give her back?

Outside, Lark finally moved from her spot on the sidelines, inching closer to the boys. Her small hands were clenched, her whole body tense. But then something shifted. She moved fast, picking up a handful of snow and flinging it with surprising accuracy at Tucker, hitting him square in the face. He toppled over, flat on his back in the snow. For a second, Lark froze, a look of horror on her face. Then Tucker burst out laughing, and she relaxed, a small smile appearing on her lips.

That's when I saw Gremlin plow through the snow toward Lark. The ball of fluff kept falling in the deep patches of snow. Her tiny white paws sank straight through the thick, powdery blanket, and I watched as Gremlin disappeared completely into the holes of the kids' bootprints. All I could see was the tip of her tiny tail, flitting like a flag lost in a snowdrift. Then Gremlin leaped—well, tried to—and promptly fell face-first into another patch of snow. She was making progress, albeit slow progress, toward Lark. Gremlin finally made it past the last deep footprint and tumbled into a much shallower bit of snow, resulting in a puffball of kitten fur and powder. She shook herself off, made a beeline for Lark, weaving between her boots and brushing up against her shins.

Lark blinked as Gremlin climbed up Lark's jeans, her claws finding purchase on Lark's clothes, though they must have tickled because the girl started giggling—an actual, honest-to-Goddess giggle. The sound was so genuine, so raw, it floated on the cold air around her, ringing out like a bell that we could hear even in the study.

Gremlin had given her approval of the girl. I turned back to the room.

"We're not giving the girl back," I said. All eyes turned toward me. "At least not until we find out what is going on with her Pack. She's here. We'll protect her until we see a reason not to."

"Mai—" Ryan started, but I knew he was going to say that I was acting rashly and jumping into decisions again.

"I know how dangerous this could be. But we can't turn her away."

I expected resistance from his brothers, but Sam, Derek, and Mason remained quiet.

Ryan exhaled slowly, then nodded once, finally letting out a low sigh. "Alright," he said. "We'll do it your way. We'll protect her."

CHAPTER TEN

MAXWELL

The kitchen was modern, warm, and bright. The rich scent of chocolate and spices filled the air, but I barely noticed any of it. My attention was fixed on the woman moving around the space, the one who was doing her best to pretend she didn't know exactly who I was.

Sylvie.

Five years hadn't changed her much. Her hair was shorter now, but she still moved with that same quiet grace. She still had that stubborn set to her jaw when she was concentrating, though. The way she was concentrating now, very deliberately not meeting my eyes as she pulled mugs down from a cabinet.

"Hot chocolate?" she asked, her voice carefully neutral. "Or would you prefer coffee?"

"Coffee is fine," I watched her reach for ground coffee beans and noticed the slight tremor in her hands. "You know, it's funny, you remind me of this girl I met in a bar just outside of Portland. She made me coffee too, though I seem to remember she liked adding whiskey to it. It was a little place called The Rusty Nail. You ever been there?"

Her movements faltered for just a second. Barely noticeable, but I caught it.

"The Rusty Nail?" Her tone was light, disinterested. Too light. Too disinterested. "I can't say I know it."

"You sure about that?" I leaned against the counter, close enough that I could catch her scent—vanilla and something wild underneath, just like I remembered. "Because I distinctly remember drinking with a beautiful werewolf there. Right before she helped me take down one of the most dangerous gangs in the Pacific Northwest."

Sylvie's hands stilled on the counter. For a long moment, she didn't move, didn't speak. Then, very quietly, "That was a long time ago."

"Not that long." I kept my voice low, aware of werewolf hearing in the house. "Five years, two months, and about sixteen days. But who's counting?"

She turned then, finally meeting my eyes. "What do you want, Maxwell?"

The directness of her stare hit me, and I almost took a step back. Those eyes—warm brown with flecks of gold—were exactly as I remembered them. I'd spent months searching for those eyes after she disappeared.

"I want to know why you ran." The words came out rougher than I intended. "After everything—after that night—you just vanished. Why? I thought something had happened to you."

"I had to disappear," she said, wrapping her arms around herself. "After what I did ... giving up Grace's location ... I couldn't—"

"You saved lives," I cut in. "That gang was out of control. Your sister was out of control. They had already killed three humans. They were going to kill a fuckload more people if we didn't stop them. You did the right thing."

"Did I?" Her laugh was bitter. "I betrayed my own sister."

"No. Your sister betrayed you when she dragged you into that situation. She was supposed to protect you, not expose you to all that." I stepped closer, close enough to see the faint freckles across her nose. I remembered tracing those with my fingertips. "The gang is still in jail, where they belong. Nobody else got hurt. That's because of you."

Sylvie shook her head, turning back to the counter. "That's not how I remember it."

"No? Well, if you had stayed around after, I would have made damn sure that was what you remembered."

She looked up at me, a fucking adorable little wrinkle between her eyes. "Why?"

"Because what you did was fucking brave. Because the night I spent with you was the best night of my life. Because you deserve to be told what a fucking incredible person you are every minute of every day."

"I wasn't brave. I was terrified. And then we had that night together and ... and I told you everything and ..." She broke off, her cheeks flushing.

"You know why it was the best night of my life?"

She shook her head.

"Not because my brother and I had been trying to shut that gang down for months, and you gave up the information that enabled us to finally get that done. But because for one night, I got to spend time with this girl who was wild and free and so fucking full of life. She was the strongest girl I had ever met. It took a fuckload of guts to do what you did."

The blush deepened on her cheeks. "I was different then."

"No." I shook my head. "You're still that same woman. You might lie to yourself and lie to the folks here, but I see her in there. She ain't gone. No matter how hard you try to cover her up or hide her away." I stepped closer, close enough that she had to tip her head back to keep looking at me. "I see you, Sylvie."

For a moment, something flickered in her eyes—a flash of the wild, free spirit I'd glimpsed that night. Then she lowered her eyes and looked away. "I need to make the coffee."

I caught her wrist gently as she reached for the mugs. "I thought I'd found the girl for me, and then she disappeared on me. I spent six months looking for you after that night." I watched her shoulders tense. "I never stopped thinking about you. Never stopped wondering where you were, if you were okay." I ran my thumb over her pulse point, felt it jump under my touch. "Finding you here ... it feels like fate."

"There's no such thing as fate." But her voice wavered.

"Then call it luck. Or Christmas magic." I smiled. "Either way, I'm not letting you disappear on me again."

She pulled her hand free, and I almost laughed at the deer-in-headlights look on her face.

"What, you thought it was over between us? Nah, babe, it's only just begun."

CHAPTER ELEVEN

SYLVIE

*A*nd just what the hell did that mean?

My wolf rubbed up against my skin. She had no problem with Maxwell chasing us. Nope. None at all. The little traitor. She remembered the way he'd looked at us that night in Portland, like we were something precious and wild and worth protecting. Not like Levi and his crew, who'd looked at me like I was just Grace's kid sister, someone to be used and discarded.

Maxwell's scent was overwhelming, filling up the kitchen with memories I'd tried so hard to forget. That night in Portland. The way his hands had felt, calloused but gentle, so different from the rough handling I'd grown used to in the gang. The freedom I'd found writhing underneath him before everything fell apart. For those few hours, I'd remembered what it felt like to be me again. Not Grace's shadow, not the gang's punching bag, just … Sylvie.

His arm brushed mine, and electricity shot through me. I missed who I used to be, missed the carefree me, the one before Levi had come into our lives, the one who hadn't been afraid to take chances. Who danced on top of bars and raced motorcycles through thunderstorms, laughing as the rain soaked through her clothes. The one who'd dreamed of opening a bakery with her sister before Grace discovered that power tasted sweeter than any dessert we could make.

My wolf was restless, pacing beneath my skin. She remembered, too. Remembered the way Maxwell had made us feel—alive, wild, free. The way he'd traced the scar on my shoulder with such tenderness, not asking about its origin but somehow understanding. The way he'd held me after, like I was something worth keeping.

I lowered my eyes to the mugs in front of me, focusing on the simple task of measuring coffee grounds. Like I had every morning for the past two years. Safe. Predictable. The complete opposite of the girl who used to spend her weekends helping Grace plan heists, heart racing with equal parts thrill and terror.

No. I couldn't go there. I had built a life here. A quiet, safe life. The Three Rivers Pack had given me sanctuary when I needed it most, asking no questions about my past. Here, I could hide in plain sight, could pretend to be nothing more than the shy housekeeper who baked cookies and kept to herself.

Boring, my wolf whispered. *Empty*.

"Sylvie." Maxwell's voice was low, rough. "Look at me."

I kept my eyes down, focusing on the coffee grounds like they held the secrets to the universe. The last time I'd looked into those eyes, I'd spilled all my secrets. Told him everything about Grace's plans, about the upcoming heist, about the innocent people who were going to get hurt. One look from him and I'd betrayed my own sister, my Pack.

"Why did you run? At least tell me that. Help me understand."

Nope. That was definitely not happening. There was no way I

could tell him that the night we spent together had changed my life. After two years as part of the biker Pack, after Levi and Grace had killed the Alphas and taken over after it became clear that Grace only wanted power and more power, and didn't give a shit how she got it or who she trampled over to get it, Maxwell had shown me kindness and tenderness and given me the best, most mind-blowing sex I've ever had. He'd shown me a glimpse of what life could be like when people cared about each other and weren't just looking out for themselves.

I'd made the decision there and then that I'd tell him anything he wanted to know, anything to stop what my Pack was doing. I couldn't tell him about the next morning, about my last meeting with Grace, or what Levi had done. About them realizing that I had betrayed them in the worst way. No, Maxwell was too good for me. I could never pollute him with the person I was. I was someone who'd done things she was deeply ashamed of, had had things done to her, who'd betrayed her own Pack, her own sister. I wasn't the sort of person who deserved to be loved after that. And anyone around me would be tarred with the same stigma. I could never do that to him.

"Look at me, Sylvie."

I couldn't. Because if I looked at him, if I let myself remember that night fully, I'd do something stupid. Like kiss him. Just one more time. To give me one more good memory to help me through the hard nights. Or maybe I'd take Wally's advice and drag Maxwell into the pantry and ...

Oh.

The thought hit me like lightning, sharp and electric. My wolf perked up, interested. The pantry was right there. It locked from the inside. And Maxwell ... Maxwell was looking at me like he wanted to devour me whole. Like he had that night in Portland when he'd made me forget everything but the feel of his hands on my skin.

What was stopping me? Really? The carefully constructed walls I'd built? The safe, predictable routine I'd hidden behind? The fear that one taste of freedom would make me crave more?

Goddess, I was so tired of being safe. I wanted to be that wild, free spirit again. Just one more time. I wanted to be the girl who'd laughed without fear, who'd believed in the possibility of happiness. I didn't want to be the reliable, shy housekeeper. I wanted to throw caution to the wind …

Before I could think too hard about it, I grabbed Maxwell's wrist and yanked him toward the pantry. His eyes widened in surprise, but he followed, a cocky grin spreading across his face as I pulled him inside and clicked the lock.

"Well, well," he murmured, backing me against the shelves. "There she is. The girl I remember."

"Shut up and kiss me."

He laughed, soft and deep, but then his mouth was on mine, and I wasn't thinking about anything anymore. Just the taste of him, the feel of his hands sliding under my shirt, the way my wolf howled in triumph as we finally, finally got what we'd been craving for five long years.

A bag of flour tumbled down somewhere to our left, but I didn't care. "Fuck, babe," Maxwell growled as I worked at his belt. "You have no idea how many times I've thought about this."

"Less talking," I demanded, shoving his jeans down his hips. "More touching."

His laugh turned into a groan as I wrapped my hand around him.

"Yes, ma'am."

For the first time in years, I felt alive. Wild. Free. Like the girl I used to be before everything went wrong. Maxwell's hands were everywhere, and I wanted more. Needed more.

He seemed to read my mind, yanking off my jeans and panties and lifting me easily. I wrapped my legs around his waist as he pressed me harder against the shelves. Something else fell—cinnamon and the dried orange by the smell—the clash of spice in the air making everything more intense.

The shelf behind me dug into my back, but I barely noticed. All I could focus on was him—his touch, his scent, the way his body fit perfectly against mine.

"Now," I breathed against his mouth. "Please, now."

His hands slid up my thighs, gripping them tightly as he ground against me. I could feel him, hard and ready, and it sent a shiver of anticipation down my spine. My wolf growled low in my chest, eager and impatient. She wanted this as much as I did.

"Max," I gasped, tearing my mouth away from his. "Please—"

He understood my plea, reaching between us. His fingers brushed against my sensitive flesh, and I jolted at the contact, a soft whimper escaping my lips. He chuckled, the sound low and husky, before positioning himself at my entrance.

Then, with one swift thrust, he was inside me.

I clung to him, my nails digging into his shoulders as he began to move. Each thrust was deep and powerful, sending waves of pleasure crashing through me.

The shelves dug into my back, and the scent of spices filled the air, but all I could focus on was Maxwell. The feel of him, the taste of him, the sounds he made as we chased our release. This was reckless and wild, and I loved every second of it.

His mouth found my neck, his teeth grazing the sensitive skin as he pounded into me. I could feel my climax building, the tension coiling tighter and tighter in my core. My breath came in short, ragged gasps, and my heart beat wildly in my chest. He was relentless, holding me up as his cock filled me completely with each stroke.

"Close," I managed to choke out, my voice barely more than a whimper. "So close—"

Maxwell increased his pace. The world around me blurred, the pleasure overwhelming and all-consuming. Then, with one final thrust, I shattered. The orgasm ripped through me, intense and explosive. I cried out, my body convulsing as wave after wave of pleasure washed over me. Maxwell followed me over the edge, his body shuddering as he found his own release.

We clung to each other, our breaths coming in ragged gasps as we rode out the aftershocks. Max pressed his forehead to mine. "Don't you dare run from me again," he whispered.

Reality crashed back in. Oh, the ever-loving Goddess. I'd just had sex in the pantry! With Maxwell Bishop. While there was a house full of werewolves with enhanced hearing just rooms away.

"Sylvie." Maxwell's voice was firm. "I can hear you panicking. Stop it."

"I just ... I don't usually ... this isn't—"

"Don't even try it. This is exactly who you are," he cut me off. "Brave enough to take what you want." He kissed me softly. "And I'm not letting you hide from it anymore."

"Max ..."

"I'm coming back for you. When this is all over, I'm coming back. And I'm going to court you properly this time. Take you on real dates. Show you that you don't have to hide who you are anymore."

My heart stuttered. "I don't know if I can—"

"You can. You will." He smiled, that dangerous, beautiful smile that had first caught my attention in that dive bar. "Because you're not just the quiet housekeeper, Sylvie. You're the woman who danced on a tabletop with me till midnight. Who takes chances. Who saves lives." He kissed me again, deep and thorough. "And I'm going to remind you of that every chance I get."

He stepped back, helping me straighten my clothes. Just before he opened the door, he turned back to me.

"And Sylvie? Next time we do this? It won't be in a pantry."

He slipped out, leaving me standing there with swollen lips and a racing heart.

I pressed a hand to my chest, feeling the wild beat there. This was crazy. This wasn't my life now, wasn't who I was anymore. But I couldn't shake the feeling that for the first time in years, maybe—just maybe—I could be that girl again. The one who wasn't afraid to live.

Chapter Twelve

RYAN

"You better come back in one piece." Mai tilted her head back just enough for me to catch the curve of her mouth—a soft yet resigned smile.

"I always do."

Mai's body leaned against the front door post, the frost on the ground crunching under her feet. She looked calm, but I could sense her restlessness crackling just below the surface. We'd pulled in everyone we could, then made our plans to shore up our defenses in case Lark's Pack came visiting. Derek, Sam, and Mason were behind Mai, ready to go. She wanted to come with us, and her need to act buzzed through our mate bond like an electric current. I needed her here, though. This was the safest place for her and the baby.

"If things go sideways before we've set the traps, the pups are going to need you here."

She didn't answer, but she didn't need to. I felt her silent agreement settle between us, a pulse of certainty through the bond.

I took a step toward her and heard her pulse speed up.

"You know, this wasn't what I had in mind for our holidays. When

I imagined tonight, I thought I'd be naked round about now."

"No." I let some heat slip into my voice. "My plan was to have had you naked for hours by now."

Mai's lips curved into a wicked smile. "I like your plan better."

"Me too. They definitely didn't involve Wally turning our house into Santa's workshop." I nipped at her neck, inhaling her scent. Goddess, she smelled incredible. "Or Maxwell Bishop showing up with a runaway pup."

"No?" Her breath hitched as I found that spot just below her ear that always made her shiver.

"You know what drives me crazy?" I murmured against her throat. "Watching you in Pack meetings, all fierce and commanding. Makes me want to drag you away and remind you who your mate is."

"As if I could forget." Her fingers twisted in my shirt, pulling me closer. "You're not exactly subtle about it."

"Neither are you, baby." I caught her wrist as her hand slipped lower. "Especially not when you do that thing with your leg under the table."

Her grin was wicked. "What thing?"

"You know exactly what thing."

"Hmm," Mai pressed closer, tilting her head up. "You mean that thing I did last week in the meeting with Shaw Investigations when you cut Carlito off, announced we had another meeting to get to and picked me up and carried my out of there?"

"Yes. That thing. I also remember we didn't make it to the bedroom before Derek arrived wanting to discuss the border patrol schedules?"

She sighed. "Yeah, I guess it's not just today. This whole Alpha gig is causing chaos with our sex life."

"About that. I've been thinking—"

I jerked my head up to the sound of boots crunching snow. Wally was marching toward us, looking like he'd just raided a goddamn army surplus store. His combat vest—if you could call it that—was at least two sizes too big, and he seemed to have strapped on every tactical gadget known to man. Straps dangled precariously from his gear, one of them dragging along in the snow, and to top it off, he had a bright red tennis racket slung over his shoulder like it was a katana.

"Oh, for fuck's sake," I muttered, pinching the bridge of my nose, as Derek strolled round the side of the house and headed toward us.

"I am locked and loaded, people!" Wally declared as he planted one hand on his hip. "Who's ready to go wreak some havoc? That's right, bitches! We are!"

He adjusted his tennis racket, sticking the handle close to his chest with all the seriousness of a seasoned warrior—except for the fact that, well, he wasn't.

Derek stopped beside me and leaned in, his voice low. "Locked and loaded with what? Tequila and snacks?"

I couldn't help it—a chuckle slipped out before I could stop it.

Wally shot us both a sharp look, narrowing his eyes at Derek. "Hey, don't you knock tequila and snacks. They are vital supplies on any mission, I'll have you know! You're going to thank me in two hours when you are freezing your tushie off, and you get the munchies."

Maxwell walked out of the front door, took one look at Wally, and froze. "What the actual fuck?"

I crossed my arms and turned to Maxwell, meeting his gaze with one of my own, making no effort to soften it. "He's our secret weapon."

Maxwell blinked, then glanced back at Wally again. Wally skipped forward, patted Maxwell's leather jacket, and winked. "Don't worry, I'm like a ninja. No one sees me coming."

"With a red fucking tennis racket? Really?"

Maxwell turned to look at me. I shrugged. Wally was ours, and if he wanted to help out with a red fucking racket, so be it.

I cleared my throat. "Alright, Wally, you're with Waylen and Mason," I said. "Check the perimeter and set up Waylen's box of toys. No one gets in or out without us knowing about it."

Waylen, who had just emerged from the house with his laptop bag awkwardly slung over his shoulder, stared at the tactical nightmare that was Wally. "Okay, dude, I'll take the tech; you handle the tennis."

I turned as more people appeared on the porch.

"Jase, Carlito, you're covering the northern point. Evelyn and Shya, take the west. Derek, Sam—southern entrance. And Maxwell, you're with me." I wanted to keep a close eye on him.

We split up, some of us on foot, others heading out in the SUV's.

I led Maxwell out past where the compound walls used to be. It had been Mai's idea to tear down the walls, and despite my initial reluctance, I had to admit it was a good one. We weren't the Alphas tucked away from the rest of the Pack anymore, safe behind the walls. We led by example, with people able to drop in whenever they needed us, and weekly BBQs for the whole Pack in front of the Alpha House. It had strengthened the Pack bonds. Something we had all desperately needed after the shitshow that was Jem and Hayley's partnership and then the disaster that was Brock.

We turned left toward the eastern perimeter, away from the twinkling Christmas lights. The moon—waxing gibbous, almost full—cast a pale, ominous light over the landscape. I could feel my wolf stir at the sight of it.

Maxwell walked beside me, silent but alert. I glanced at him from the corner of my eye, studying the easy confidence in his stride, how his every movement seemed deliberate.

"You done this sort of thing before?" I asked him.

"Set traps or go up against a werewolf Pack?"

"Either."

"I'm sure you've done a background check on me," he said evenly, his eyes never leaving the path ahead. "You know I grew up in the gang. So this? This isn't even the half of the things I've done before."

That I could believe.

"Here's the deal, Bishop. If you're going to fight with us, I need to know we can trust you."

"I get that."

"But trust takes time, and time isn't something we have much of," I added, my voice low. "So, until we know more about this Pack—the one hunting Lark—you stay close out here. We work together. No surprises."

"I didn't come here to make problems," he said, his tone sharpening slightly. "I came because I owe my brother and because I figured Lark would be safer here than anywhere else. But you should know that I'm not gonna stand down if her Pack does turn up. I promised I'd protect Lark with my life, and I meant it."

"And you should know that we're going out on a limb for you and the pup right now. My Pack comes first. You do anything to fuck with us, if this is some sort of trap by Ronnie, I will rip your fucking head off."

He studied me for a moment, his face not showing any emotion.

Then he nodded. "Fair enough."

I still couldn't get a read on him, and it pissed me off. Time to push him.

"You smell of Sylvie."

His foot hesitated, just for a moment, before it landed on the snow. *Got him.*

"Yeah?"

"Yeah. You hurt her, and I won't just rip your head off; I'll take you apart limb by limb. Make sure you're alive for it, too."

I caught a flair of anger in his scent, but he tampered it down quick. I was impressed, not many humans had that sort of control, especially around Shifters.

"I have no intention of hurting her. Quite the opposite."

Oh, really?

"Sylvie is special to us. She might be a werewolf, but she's delicate. She's been hurt in the past, and you need to tread real careful with her. I'm not the only one who'll go for your throat if you put a foot wrong."

I caught a trace of a smile cross his face.

"I'm well aware of how special she is. And Sylvie will be the first to know my intentions. After that, I figure it's her choice. Not yours."

I stopped, letting the green sheen of my wolf flash across my eyes and a low growl enter my voice. "I'm her Alpha. You're human; you're not part of our Pack, never will be. You have no understanding of how a Pack works and the extent to which we'll go to protect our own. Sylvie is ours. She wants to fuck you, that's up to her. But you do anything to hurt her or this Pack, and we, every motherfucking one of us, will turn on you. We understand each other?"

Maxwell hesitated for a moment but didn't back down. He nodded. "We do."

Good. After this was over, I'd tell Mai what was going on and ask her to talk to Sylvie and make sure she was okay with Maxwell sniffing around. I hoped it was a one-time thing. Werewolf and human pairs were not unheard of, but they were discouraged. And Ronnie fucking Bishop's brother, of all people? If this was something Sylvie wanted, it was going to get complicated fast.

Chapter Thirteen

Mai

"No, no! You gotta press X to jump, then triangle to do the special move!" Tucker bounced on his knees, controller forgotten in his lap as he watched Lark struggle with the buttons. "You almost had it that time!"

Lark's face was scrunched in concentration, her fingers awkward on the controller. "There are too many buttons."

"Here." Ben scooted closer to her on the floor. "Watch me first." He gently took the controller. "See? X is jump, circle is dodge, and if you press them together ..." His character on screen executed a perfect aerial combo.

Lark's eyes widened. "How did you learn all this?"

"Practice." Ben shrugged. "And Thomas taught me. He's really good at games, but last week, I even beat him!"

A small smile tugged at Lark's lips. "Really?"

Ben ducked his head, but I caught the pleased flush on his cheeks. He handed the controller back to her. This time, he pointed to each button as he explained, his voice patient. "Just focus on jumping first."

Lark's tongue poked out slightly as she concentrated. Her character jumped, wobbled, then managed to land on a platform.

"You did it!" Tucker cheered, throwing his hands in the air.

"Okay," Lark said, squaring her shoulders. "Show me how to do that special move thing again."

I left them to it and headed to the kitchen, where I could watch the steam rise lazily from the kettle as it began to boil. Ever since I got pregnant, I liked watching it; it helped me think. Sylvie had left a note on the table saying she was popping home but would be back soon. The room smelled of cinnamon and orange, and the soft, rhythmic hum of the water heating filled the empty space. The sound was a welcome break from the thoughts going around in my mind. I missed Ryan, felt the strain in our mate bond that he wasn't nearby. I worried about Lark's Pack, and if they attacked now, when the alarms weren't in place... The House was vulnerable. We were vulnerable. We didn't know enough, and that was partly my fault.

Had I done the right thing?

The question circled over and over like a broken record. I'd told Ryan we were going to protect Lark even though we barely knew anything about her or the Pack that wanted her back. The decision had rolled off my tongue without hesitation. But now, standing here alone in the quiet, I was starting to worry that perhaps it had been another of those rash decisions that Ryan was so concerned about.

Protect the pup.

My wolf had no doubts. Good to know.

I poured the hot water into the cup, watching the dark tendrils of the ginger and peppermint tea unfurl from the bag as I stirred the spoon slowly, the scent catching the updrafts in the room and swirling into the air. What if I was making decisions I wouldn't have before I was pregnant?

Caught in my own thoughts, I barely noticed Wally gliding into the kitchen until I heard his familiar, affectionate drawl.

"Sweetie, I swear, if you stir that tea any more, it's going to turn into a hurricane in that cup."

I jumped. "Shit, Wally! I thought you were out laying traps."

He perched himself on one of the stools near the counter and propped his chin up on his hand, watching me like an amused but concerned parent. "I was. We got back five minutes ago. The others are still out. It's not like you to not hear us come in. You need to tell Wally what's got you all twisted up like an origami wolf."

I plastered on a smile and turned to face him. "It's nothing, really. I'm sorry this birthday Christmas for Ben isn't turning out they way you thought it would. Is he okay?"

Wally waved a dismissive hand. "Pish posh, don't even worry about that! This party may have had a few...hiccups, but I wanted to make it memorable for Ben, and that it certainly is."

"Well, it's his birthday until midnight. So, we have until then to get this whole thing resolved and the celebrations back on track." We could do it. We had to. I didn't want to let Wally or Ben down. "How's Lark settling in out there?"

Wally tilted his head to one side. "Lark had those two boys wrapped around her finger within thirty seconds of walking in the front door. My bet is they'd lay down their lives for her in a heartbeat. So, Lark is gonna be just fine. It's you I'm worried about."

"Me?"

"Yes, you, missy. You know what I'm talking about, too, so stop acting all innocent and cheerful when I know you have a dark storm hanging over your head. So, spill."

"Honestly, there's nothing—" I started but was cut off by Sofia bursting through the kitchen door.

"Oh, thank Goddess, there's tea," Sofia said, making a beeline for the kettle. "I'm adding whiskey to it, though. I need an escape."

"An escape? From what, or who?" Wally asked with a grin, then held up one hand. "No, don't tell me! My guess is the very hot, muscular Shaw brother who only has eyes for you."

Sofia shot him a look that could have melted steel. "Not helping."

"Speaking of not helping," Wally turned back to me, "our Alpha here was just about to tell us what's bothering her."

Sofia's attention snapped to me, her eyes narrowing as she studied my face. "I knew something was up. You've got that crinkle between your eyes that you always get when you're overthinking things."

I reached up to rub the spot between my eyebrows. "I do not have a crinkle!"

"Girl, you have the mother of all crinkles right now," Sofia said, hopping onto the counter. "You might as well spill it. You know it won't go until you do. So, what's going on in that head of yours?"

I sighed, looking between my two friends. "I ... I'm not sure I made the right decision back there."

"About Lark?" Sofia asked, her head in the pantry as she grabbed a bottle of Aberlour whiskey. "What the hell happened in here? It looks like an earthquake hit!" She inhaled deeply, then sneezed. "Shit! Never mind. I think I know."

Wally narrowed his eyes at Sofia, then swung his gaze back to me. "Enough distractions. You're worried about Lark."

I shrugged. "Taking her in ... it puts our Pack at risk, and I'm not sure whether I made that call because it was right or because I'm pregnant and my hormones are making me—"

"Oh, hell no," Sofia cut me off. "We are not doing the hormone blame game. I've known you since high school, Mai Parker, and you've always been a sucker for strays. Remember that three-legged squirrel you tried to hide in your locker?"

Wally looked from Sofia to me and back again. "There's a story I need to hear."

"She kept him in there for two weeks," Sofia grinned. "Fed him tuna sandwiches and tried to convince everyone the scratching and chirping was her new ringtone."

I felt my cheeks flush. "That was different—"

"Was it?" Sofia raised an eyebrow. "What about Gremlin?"

Okay, maybe she had a point.

"You saw something that needed help, and you jumped in to protect it. That's who you've always been. The only difference now is you have the power to actually do something about it."

"But what if I'm not thinking clearly—"

"Oh, darling," Wally interrupted, his tone half-relieved and half-exasperated. "That is horseshit."

"Horseshit?"

"Yes, horseshit. Baloney. Utter nonsense." Wally stood up and started pacing, his hands gesturing wildly. "You're not making these decisions because you've gone soft. You're making them because you give a damn. You've always cared. Look at Korrin's rogues. You offered them a way to be part of a Pack again. Amara and Ben? You found them a home, a way to be safe. Face it. You collect strays. Probably because you were one and know what it's like to be on the outside.

That's what makes you *you*. It's what makes you a good leader. Hell, it's why people follow you and Ryan. But if you think for one second it's because you're pregnant and somehow too emotional or hormonal, then forgive me when I say—" He waved his hands theatrically in the air. "Absolute fucking horseshit."

"He's right." Sofia nodded, reaching over to squeeze my hand. "You need to trust your instincts, not second-guess them. And if anyone tries to come after that little girl, they'll have to go through all of us first. Even Derek's brooding ass would fight for her."

"Speaking of Derek's ass ..." Wally wiggled his eyebrows.

"Don't you dare start," Sofia warned, but I caught the slight flush in her cheeks.

"I saw you checking out said ass when he was rehanging the Christmas lights Gremlin knocked off the tree earlier."

"I was not! I was ... supervising the decoration placement."

"You most certainly were supervising the placement of his decorations."

I couldn't help laughing at the look on Sofia's face.

Sofia groaned and buried her face in her hands. "I hate you both."

"No, you don't," Wally sang. "You love us. Almost as much as you love Derek's—"

"Finish that sentence, and I will end you," Sofia threatened.

Something warm settled in my chest, easing some of the tension there. These two ... they always knew how to pull me out of my head.

"Face it, Mai," Sofia said, turning serious again. "You're a good Alpha *because* you care. Not in spite of it. And being pregnant doesn't change that—it just gives you one more reason to fight for what's right."

"Besides," Wally added, "what will Ryan do if you start out-brooding him? Leave the dramatic worrying to him, alright? It's better for his whole mysterious-and-grumpy-Alpha aesthetic."

"True," I murmured. "Can't take that away from him. He does enjoy it so much."

"Almost as much as Derek enjoys pretending he's not staring at Sofia," Wally quipped.

"That's it!" Sofia launched herself off the counter, but Wally was already dancing away, cackling as he dodged her swat.

I watched them chase each other around the kitchen, their laughter filling the space and felt my wolf settle. I'd found this, my family. Was it so bad if I wanted others to find it, too?

Chapter Fourteen

RYAN

We used the trails with the most compacted snow—the ones our wolves used to navigate through the forest—and worked in silence, setting traps and silent alarms rigged to trigger if anyone crossed the boundaries. Maxwell wasn't just precise—he was fast. Efficient. He might be a lawyer now, but he hadn't forgotten the skills he'd grown up with. He pulled thin wire from his pack, the kind that would be nearly invisible against the snow, especially in the dark.

"I'm impressed with the equipment," Maxwell said, kneeling to secure one end to a sturdy tree trunk. We were connecting all the wires to small charges—nothing lethal, but enough bang to disorient enhanced hearing. "This is state-of-the-art stuff. I don't think even the military has these latest chargers."

"We have our sources." Derek had contacts all across the intelligence world and usually managed to get us new equipment before it hit the market.

"The last time I used something like this was against a Pack of Shifters who had developed a taste for human meat."

I raised an eyebrow. "Man-eaters?"

"Let's just say being Ronnie's brother meant dealing with all sorts of supernatural shit." He threaded the wire through a clever mechanism that would trigger the charge. "The trick with these is to layer the defenses. First line should be early warning—simple stuff that lets us know they're coming. Second line needs to slow them down, make them cautious."

I nodded, impressed despite myself. "And the third line?"

"That's where we get creative." He pulled out what looked like small metal discs. "These are filled with powdered silver. Won't kill a werewolf, but it'll hurt like hell and mess with their sense of smell. Picked up that trick from a hunter in Louisiana."

We worked methodically, setting up three defensive rings around the property. The outer ring was pure surveillance—pressure plates buried under the snow, motion sensors in the trees. The middle ring combined trip wires with those silver charges, positioned to create bottlenecks that would force any attackers into predetermined paths.

"The inner ring is the most important," I said, surveying our work. "We need to funnel them where we want them."

Maxwell nodded. "You're thinking about the clearing by the east side of the Alpha House?"

"Yeah. If we get enough warning, it has good sight lines, and we can position our enforcers in the trees. Anyone who makes it through gets bottlenecked right into our strongest fighters."

"Smart." Maxwell checked the tension on another wire. "But if they're anything like the Packs I've dealt with before, they'll be expecting something like that."

I resisted the urge to grind my teeth. I was sure Ronnie knew exactly what Pack we'd be dealing with. If he had shared that info with his brother, we could have put Waylen on the case, and we'd know for sure what they were capable of. "You've fought many werewolf Packs?"

He was quiet for a moment as I tested the mechanism I'd just set one more time, before he answered.

"More than I'd like. Back when I was with the gang, we had … territorial disputes with several Packs. They'd try to move product through our territory; we'd push back. Things would get messy." His jaw tightened. "Lost some good people learning how to fight them … you … effectively."

"That's why you left?"

"Part of it." He stood, brushing snow from his knees. "Learned pretty quick that in that kind of fight, you either get really good at adapting, at strategy, or you end up dead.

I watched him work, noting how his hands never hesitated, how each movement was precise and practiced. This wasn't just someone who'd picked up a few tricks. This was experience earned the hard way.

The traps were psychological. Werewolves rely on their enhanced senses—take those away, make them doubt what they're sensing, and you've already won half the battle.

"If they come this direction, they'll cross that line," I said, nodding toward the last trap we'd arranged. "And when they do, they'll come hard and fast."

My wolf stirred, alert now. The woodland around us—the snow-covered trees, crisp and silent—looked peaceful. But I had the feeling that peace was a fucking mask.

Maxwell exhaled a breath through his nose, nodding. "Yeah, that's how I'd attack."

That was how I'd do it, too. Maxwell was good. I suspected he'd be deadly in a fight, but he could think strategically as well. He'd be a dangerous opponent if we ever found ourselves on opposite sides. My wolf peeked out of my eyes as I took another glance around. He sensed something out there.

"We should head back," Maxwell said, standing up once more and dusting the powdered snow from his pants.

I scanned the forest again.

"You see something?"

"No." I shook my head as my wolf lay down. "I don't like it, though."

We set off back, and as we got nearer the house, I felt the familiar warmth of the bond pulse lightly between me and Mai. I could sense her waiting, and her worry beneath her calm. I pushed back, sending her a quiet reminder that I was okay, and coming home.

I stamped off the snow from my boots just outside the door. My wolf stirred as the smell of cinnamon and Pack filled my nostrils. The others were already back.

Inside, someone had thrown more logs into the fireplace, and the flames cast flickering gold light across the floor. I could hear the sounds of laughter from one direction—Ben and Tucker were showing Lark how to play street fighter on the PlayStation, and from the sounds of it, she was kicking their asses. Jase, one foot propped casually against the doorframe, was keeping watch. He nodded silently as we came in, but I was getting definite pissed-off vibes coming from him. My guess? It had something to do with Amara sitting on Cameron's lap in the lounge.

Mai appeared from the kitchen, carrying a jug of what smelled like mulled wine, the scent of cloves, cinnamon, and oranges drifting toward me. Nothing could cover her scent, though, the honeysuckle, mint, and dried aspen leaves hitting something directly in my core. My eyes met hers, and a pulse zipped along our mate bond. She smiled at me, her face lighting up, and I felt my wolf sigh with relief. We were on edge whenever we were away from her and our pup. I thought it would get easier with time, but so far, this urge to have Mai in sight at all times had only gotten worse. I strode over and kissed her, my lips capturing hers. She felt hot to touch, and I wanted to order everyone to get the hell out of our house so I could fuck her senseless.

Wally appeared behind Mai, his frilly pink apron tied around his waist and a plate full of wolf-shaped gingerbread cookies in his hands. "Oooh, you guys need to get a room!"

I wanted to throttle him. Me and Mai were never gonna get some alone time at this rate. I glared at Wally. "I don't need a room. I have a house. This house."

Wally grinned at me. "Yeah, but we've decided that no one is going to war on an empty stomach. That's a new rule in this Pack."

"Is that so?"

Mai bit her lower lip, and I knew exactly who "we" was.

"I thought you were locked and loaded?"

"I am locked and loaded," Wally waved the plate at me, "with sugar, caffeine, and enough gingerbread cookies to see us through at least a minor siege."

"Did I hear someone mention cookies?" Mason's voice came from the lounge.

"I could eat cookies!" Shya chimed in. I knew they were having a bumpy ride taking over the Bridgetown Pack, what with Camille going AWOL to deal with her grief, leaving them to raise Shya's younger brothers, Henry and Tucker, plus half the Pack still unsure about a Three Rivers werewolf leading them, but I'd still never seen Mason so happy.

Wally tossed me a see-I-told-you-so look, then swept past me to deliver them to his troops.

"Thomas, Amara, and Cameron got all the med supplies moved over," Mai told me, snaking her free arm around my waist.

We'd decided that Thomas would use the spare rooms here as a med ward until this was over. Lark was here, so the Alpha House was where her old Pack would come looking for her. If there was a battle, it didn't make sense for Thomas to try to move anyone who got injured back to his house.

"Good."

I grasped her hand and led her to the lounge. For a moment, we just stood there, watching our Pack fill up this warm, festive space, gingerbread wolves scattered across counters now, snow-dusted boots by the door, and the hum of music somewhere in the background.

"This feels ... strange," she admitted as she leaned into me. "Like we're waiting for both Christmas and war."

"It's a delicate balance," I said, dropping a kiss on her temple.

Her hand squeezed mine. "Any sign of them?"

"Not yet. But they'll come. And soon."

That's what I would do.

Chapter Fifteen

DEREK

"**D**on't even think about it," I growled from the doorway, watching Sofia methodically checking the throwing knives.

I had caught her scent before I reached the weapons room—vanilla and jasmine mixed with the sharp tang of silver from the blades she was handling. My wolf surged forward, desperate to be closer to her. I ruthlessly shoved him back down. This wasn't the time.

She didn't turn around. "I don't know what you're talking about."

Stubborn woman. My jaw clenched as I watched her fingers dance over the silver-tipped blades. Every protective instinct I had was screaming at me to grab her, lock her somewhere safe, and keep her far away from tonight's fight. But I knew better than to try that with Sofia. She'd probably stab me with one of those knives she was fondling.

"You're planning to fight."

She turned then, raising one perfect eyebrow at me. "Well, yeah. That's generally what happens when someone threatens your Pack. You fight."

Fucking hell, she was beautiful when she was being defiant. Which was pretty much always.

"You're not fighting tonight." The words came out harsher than I intended.

She laughed, short and sharp. "Excuse me?"

"Sofia—"

"No, please, continue telling me what I can and can't do. I do so love it when you go all caveman on me. You might have noticed how I swoon at your feet every time you do it."

I swear she was going to drive me to an early grave.

Memories of that night at the fairground flashed through my mind—our first date, before everything had gone to shit, her body pressed against mine, the taste of her skin, the way she'd whispered my name. Then the wall covered in her photos in that fucking cabin in the woods. They'd found her. Were watching her. Because of me.

"This isn't a joke," I snapped.

"Do you see me laughing?"

We stood there, glaring at each other. She had no idea what she was dealing with. The people hunting me—hunting her now—they wouldn't hesitate to use her. The thought of them touching her made my wolf howl with rage.

"You know why you can't be out there," I said, fighting to keep my voice steady.

"Actually, I don't. Because you won't tell me any damn thing." She turned back to the weapons, but I caught the anger in her voice. "All I know is that sometimes you look at me like ... like ..."

Like you're my everything. Like I'd tear apart anyone who tried to hurt you. Like I'm terrified of what loving you might cost us both.

I moved closer, my steps silent. The need to touch her, to explain everything, warred with the knowledge that the closer I got to her, the more danger she was in.

"It's not safe."

She spun to face me, and suddenly she was too close. Close enough that I could see the flecks of gold in her eyes, count each freckle across her nose. Close enough that it took everything in me not to pull her into my arms.

"Oh, really? And it took you how many years of military training to work out a battle with another Pack might not be safe?"

That hadn't been what I'd meant, but I didn't correct her.

"Look, Sofia. You're just gonna have to ..." Fuck, she licked her lips, and my mind went completely blank. Then the image of her lips licking my cock rose like a gigantic neon sign in my head.

"Have to what?"

My mind snapped back. Fuck! I had to make sure she didn't fight. "Listen to me—"

"I don't think so, Derek. Last time I checked, you have no authority over me."

"I'm your ..."

Mate. I desperately wanted to acknowledge it. My wolf was howling it, for fuck's sake.

"Beta. I'm your Beta. So technically, I do have authority over you."

She narrowed her eyes at me and put her hands on her hips. "You try that, and I'll go over your head to Mai. The *Alpha* will let me fight."

Shit. She was bluffing. *Wasn't she?*

"Sofia—"

"I'm fighting. You can either help me prep, or you can leave. Your choice."

For a moment, I thought about arguing. My jaw was clenched so tight I doubted I could get any words out. She grabbed a set of throwing knives, strapping them to her thigh. The movement drew my eyes to her legs, and I had to force myself to look away. Normally, werewolves didn't use weapons. Guns were considered cowardly; our wolves were our weapons. But if she had to fight, anything to give Sofia an advantage would get my approval.

"I could take you home and lock you in the panic room."

Before I could blink, she had a knife pressed against my cock. "Try it. I dare you."

The Sofia I'd gone on that first date with, the barista from the Bottley Bar, would not have been able to get a knife so close to me. I'd suspected for a while now that she'd been training with someone, but how and when they were meeting—or even if they still were—I had no idea.

"Nice move." I stepped back, and at the same time, my hand circled her wrist, twisting gently until she dropped the knife. I caught it with my other hand, flipped it, and handed it back to her. "I've seen you practice with these. Your stance is off. You favor your right side too much."

She blinked. "I practice at night. In my back room. That's kinda creepy, Derek."

I didn't give a fuck if it was creepy or not; I had eyes on her all the time now. The guys who were after her might try to grab her at any time.

"You need to adjust your stance, like this."

I took her hand and put it in the correct position. Having her this close was fucking torture. The smell of her, the warmth of her body—it was all I could do not to pull her against me and kiss that look of anger off her face.

A loud bang echoed from upstairs, followed by Wally shouting something about tennis rackets and battle stations.

"Be careful out there tonight. I can't always be around to protect you."

She tilted her head to one side and glowered at me. "No one asked you to, Derek. And it's about time it penetrated your thick skull—I don't need you to protect me. I can do that all by myself."

She had no idea. No fucking idea about the men who were coming after me. But I didn't want to scare her. No, I decided when I found her photos in the cabin that I wouldn't let them take away what was important to Sofia. If I locked her away or took her someplace to hide, away from her work, her business, her family, her friends, she'd never forgive me. They were coming after me because of what I did, and I was fucking sure I wasn't going to let that spill over and affect the life Sofia had built herself. She deserved so much better than that, than me.

I turned to leave, then paused in the doorway. Fuck it. "And Sofia?"

"Yeah?"

"When this is over ... We're gonna talk. About everything."

Her heartbeat quickened—I could hear it from across the room. "I'm not interested in anything you have to say, Derek. Haven't you got that by now?"

I couldn't blame her, but I fucking hated that I'd made her hate me. "Tough."

I left before I could say anything else, before I could give in to the urge to tell her everything. About the mission that went wrong, about the people hunting me, about how every time I pushed her away, it felt like I was tearing out a piece of my own soul.

First, we had to survive tonight.

Chapter Sixteen

Mai

I had the feeling that my best chance of getting Lark to open up was if Maxwell was there, but there was no way Ryan was leaving me alone with Maxwell. So, I led the four of us to the study. Lark was stuck to Maxwell's side, her small hand back to gripping his jacket. Again, I got the impression she was anchoring him to her so she could protect him more easily. Her eyes skated across me and Ryan nervously. She didn't trust us. Smart kid.

Ryan closed the door, locking out the sound of Tucker and Ben arguing over what game they were going to play next.

How to approach this? I could go in in Alpha-mode, be authoritative, and demand some answers. I knew that was probably how Ryan would handle this. Sofia's words to trust my instincts echoed in my mind.

Lark's eyes, wide with uncertainty, flicked toward the towering walls of shelves behind me, taking in the sheer volume of books. She didn't move, but her posture shifted ever so slightly. Ah, she was curious. That was a good sign.

"I work here a lot. So did my brother when it was his study. We both like to read. What about you, Lark? Do you read?"

Lark lowered her eyes and shook her head. "My mom was teaching me to read, before ..." She swallowed, shot a quick look at Maxwell, then continued, "Ronnie is teaching me now. I'm no good at it. But I want to read big books. Smart people read big books."

I tilted my head to one side. "People get smart in different ways. I know lots of smart people who don't read books."

She scrunched up her face, as if thinking about this. "But I like books. I want to be one of the smart people who get their smarts from books."

Maybe we should create a library for the Three Rivers kids? I'd have to talk to Wally and Thomas about it; something like that would be right up their street.

"Well, you're welcome to borrow any of the books here, anytime."

She jerked her head toward me. "Really?"

I smiled back at her. "Yes, really."

She stood frozen for a moment, then dashed toward the bookshelves, her eye scanning over the books. None of these were children's books, but I had a feeling that didn't matter to her right now. The fact that she had been given access to all these books was what was important.

Ryan sat down on the couch near the window. He was distancing himself as much as possible. Giving me space to try to talk to Lark. I shot him a grateful look. He knew we were short on time, but we couldn't rush this.

"Lark, Maxwell told us about your parents and sister."

I watched as her little body stiffened.

"You know, I lost my parents when I was young too."

Lark turned to face me as surprise flickered over her expression for a brief second.

"It's hard to talk about," I continued. "But I also know that sometimes, it can help."

She glared at me. "Will talking bring them back?"

"No—"

"So, what's the point?"

I looked at her and saw a kid barely hanging on. She had stuffed her grief into a box and slammed the lid on it. There was no way she wanted to risk opening it back up. I knew because that was exactly what I'd done.

"You know, Ryan lost his mom at the same time my parents died, and I found it helps me to know that he really understands how I feel."

Lark's eyes flickered to Ryan and then back to me.

"I know it's scary to talk about the bad things." I kept my voice calm. "Scary to feel those emotions. But I promise you, Lark, you're safe here. We want to help—you and Ronnie and Maxwell here. And whether you tell us more now or not, we'll protect you, but it would help us to do that if we knew what happened."

She softened just a little, and I could almost see something begin to crack.

"No one's going to hurt you here," I added softly. "No one's going to force you to do anything you don't want to do."

"I ... I don't ..." Her voice was angry and fragile at the same time. She looked at Maxwell, who reached down and gave a quick squeeze to her shoulder.

Finally, Lark took a breath. "My Pack ..." she trailed off.

Okay, maybe she needed a little nudge to get started. "Do you know the name of your Pack? Or your Alphas?"

She stopped and swallowed hard. "Yes. We're ... *they're* the Knox Pack. My old Alphas. Gabrielle and Artie. That's their names. They said my parents had been specially chosen to try a new medication, that if they took it, they would be in the first wave of a new type of Shifter."

My stomach tightened. "Lark, do you remember what the medication looked like?"

"They were pills. Red pills. And they ... they had these little waves on them. I thought they should be blue, not red, 'coz of the waves on them. If they were blue, they would look like an ocean. I don't think it was one of the smart people who made them red."

Fuck! Red pills. With a wave.

Ripple.

If Lark's Alphas were involved in the ripple trade and were experimenting on their own Pack, the situation was even more dangerous than we'd imagined.

I smiled gently at Lark. "No, I don't think it was one of the smart people either."

"My mom, she didn't want to but, Gabrielle and Artie said it was for the good of the Pack. That it would help us all be stronger. Dad told her they had to obey."

"So they took them?"

She nodded. "It was only supposed to be one pill a day, but soon they were taking three or four."

I shot a glance at Ryan. His jaw was tight. He knew, like I did, what that amount of ripple would do to a Shifter.

"What happened after they took them?" I asked gently.

Lark scowled. "They ... changed. They stopped being my mom and dad. They didn't want anything to do with me. They didn't want to teach me reading or math. They didn't want to play. They stopped shopping and wouldn't make me food. I don't know what I did to make them hate me. All they wanted was more pills."

Her lips trembled as tears pooled in her eyes. She was trying hard to keep them in.

I reached out and took her hand. She didn't pull away. "You did nothing wrong, Lark. They didn't hate you. They loved you. It was the pills. They made them into different people, but it had nothing to do with you, I promise."

Tears spilled out of her eyes and streamed down her face. She pulled the end of her sleeve over her free hand and used it to angrily swipe away the tears.

"Lark, is that how they died? They stopped eating?"

She shook her head. She wiped at her face again. "My mom, dad ... they were saying things. Things about not being bound to the Pack anymore ... about their bonds being impure."

Out of the corner of my eye, I saw Maxwell frown.

"The Alphas ... they came to our house." Lark's voice trembled now. "They talked to my parents, told them to stop taking the pills. But my parents ... they refused. Said they needed the pills. That it was the only thing that made them feel right. Then the Alphas went outside and ..."

Lark hesitated, defiance and fear dancing behind her eyes. Her voice dropped to a whisper. "They made a phone call. I ... I snuck out and heard Artie on the phone. The other person ... they told Artie to get rid of anyone who had taken the pills."

They were cleaning up their mess ... eradicating anyone who'd taken ripple. Alphas were supposed to protect their Pack, not use them as guinea pigs.

Lark's eyes darted toward the nearest window. "He went back inside, and Dad started shouting. I ... got scared. So I ran. I didn't know where I was going; I just wanted to get away."

"You did the right thing," I said. "You were smart. That's how you survived."

She looked up, not quite meeting my gaze but keeping her teary eyes fixed on my nose. "But I left them. I heard their screams. I left them to ... to die."

"No, sweetheart. There was nothing you could have done. If you had stayed, you wouldn't be here with us. Your parents, the ones they were before they took the pills, they would be so proud of you. You got yourself safe, and that was the most important thing you could have done."

Lark sniffed. "I ran into the forest. My wolf wanted out, so I let her. I Shifted. We knew they would come looking. That they could track me through the Pack bonds. So we went over the boundaries, the ones my dad told me never to cross."

"You did the right thing," I repeated. I didn't want her to feel guilty about any of this. "How far did you get?"

"I don't know," she replied. "After a while, I found a road. I was so tired ... I didn't care where it took me. I just ... I wanted to be somewhere safe where they couldn't track me. I thought maybe the smell from the cars would confuse them."

Smart kid.

"That's when Ronnie found me. He ... nearly ran me over with his bike. I was scared, but I was too tired to run anymore. He picked me up, put me in Tito's side-car with a blanket, and took me to his place."

"Tito?" I asked Maxwell.

"A patch holder. He's a good guy. Been there since ever since I can remember."

"Tito is nice. He and Ronnie, they brought me food and kept me warm. I stayed as a wolf for a few days," she continued, her words coming faster now. "I didn't want to Shift back. But when no one came looking for me, I thought ..."

"You thought you were safe?"

She nodded. "When I Shifted back, Ronnie asked me about what happened. I told him. He knew my Alphas. Said he would take care of it and that I could stay with him as long as I wanted. He said he could take me to a new Pack, to be with my kind. But I don't want to. I want to stay with Ronnie. He makes me safe. I didn't get a choice in what my parents did or their dying. I want a choice in this! I want to stay with Ronnie, and when I'm smart enough and big enough, I'm going to go back and kill them."

I wanted to tell her that revenge was not the answer, but hadn't I felt the same way after my parents died? I'd blamed Oliver, our old Alpha, and his schemes for getting my parents killed, and I'd hated him for it. Hell, it had started my brother, Jem, on his path to challenging Oliver and taking over the Pack.

Lark had felt safe, happy, with her parents and her Pack. Then her Alphas had forced ripple on her mom and dad, and she'd watched them change almost overnight into drug addicts and then heard her Alphas, the ones supposed to protect her, kill them. She'd had no control over what had happened. She either accepted it, accepted she was powerless, or she bided her time and plotted her revenge. At least that way, she would feel she had some agency over her life. That she could get justice for what had happened. Her anger was fueling her right now, helping her get through this. I wasn't going to take that away from her.

Where had her Pack even gotten ripple from? Who ordered Artie to cover his tracks? If Gabrielle and Artie were involved in this drug, it was likely they had contact with witches, too. What the hell were we facing? Because, face it, we would. There was no way we were giving up Lark now.

I locked eyes with Ryan. "They'll need to get rid of anyone who knows the truth. They will come for her—"

My phone buzzed in my pocket. I pulled it out to see Esme calling. "Esme?"

"There are witches in Three Rivers, Mai! They're coming!"

Chapter Seventeen

MAI

The warm light from the Christmas tree flickered softly, casting shadows that danced on the walls of the Alpha House. Silver strands of tinsel fluttered ever so slightly in the draft that came through the old windowpanes, and the smell of cinnamon, apples, and gingerbread wafted through the room. Ben was in one corner of the lounge playing charades with Tucker and Lark, but all three of them kept shooting nervous glances at us. They knew something was up, Lark especially.

Maxwell was standing off to the side, hovering near Lark. Mason, Shya, Derek, and Sam all looked relaxed but had positioned themselves around the room in the best places to fend off any attack. We were all on edge. Jase was at the fireplace, trying his best to ignore Amara and Cameron as they held hands and whispered to each other by the window.

Ryan stood, arms crossed, glowering over Waylen's shoulder at the six laptops he was running on the table as if he could make the witches appear on the screens by thought alone.

We'd had time to fill them in on the Knox Pack and their connection with ripple, along with Esme's warning that there were witches on our territory.

Unfortunately, Waylen wasn't finding anything with his state-of-the-art technology that he worshipped like a goddess.

Waylen clacked irritably at his laptop, his fingers flying over the keys as he scanned the screens. "There is nothing out there. Cameras are clear, all our traps are intact, motion detectors—nothing." His fingers paused, and his brows knit together. He looked up toward me, then over at Ryan. "Esme's sure about this?"

"Of course, I am sure," Esme replied as she swept into the room, wrapped in a winter coat several sizes too big for her. Her hair was bouncy, though tangled, and there was that flush to her face that came from walking into a warm room from the cold outside. Jem followed silently behind her. I was surprised to see him; he normally avoided the Alpha House. It wasn't easy for him to be back here, where he had lived with Hayley, where he was Alpha, where Hayley had stabbed him.

Jem's face had that blank look he got when he was hiding his thoughts and feelings, but his eyes scanned the room, taking in everything. I saw the moment his wolf saw me; his fists clenched, and his eyes flared green. Ryan stiffened, ready to jump Jem if he made any move toward me, but Jem simply nodded once at me and then at Ryan. He had it under control. I sighed. We did this dance every time Jem got near me. It was getting better, and I had hopes one day soon, his wolf would, if not forgive me, at least tolerate me so I could spend more time with my brother. The person I had grown up with seemed like a distant memory, replaced by someone darker, more dangerous. Esme was helping him, but I wanted to be there for him too.

My wolf flicked her ears. She was happy Jem was here.

Esme frowned at Waylen's computer set-up, then her eyes landed on me with a kind of urgency that knotted something tight in my gut.

"Esme, there's nothing out there," Waylen repeated.

"You're wrong. You and your toys! They are no match for witches."

"Even witches' breath, they have heat signatures, they have to walk on the ground to get places. If they were here, I'd pick them up."

"Nope. You would not. Sorry, but your wizarding skills are no match for a witch. Playing tricksy with your gadgets is child's play to us."

The expression on Waylen's face would have made me laugh if we weren't about to be attacked. I honestly thought his head was about to explode.

He opened his mouth to no doubt give an extremely explicit response, but I held up my hand. "We don't have time. Esme, are you sure?"

She turned to me and nodded.

"How many?" Ryan asked.

Esme closed her eyes and breathed deeply. I knew she wasn't scenting the witches, not like werewolves scent our prey, but more centering herself in some way.

"Two," she said flatly, opening her eyes. For a second—a fraction of a second—a flicker of panic passed over her face. "And they are strong. We will need to be tippy-toe careful."

"We can't use you, Esme," Sam said.

Everyone turned to look at him. Sam pushed off from the wall he had been leaning against and stalked to the middle of the room.

"Esme has to sit this one out," he repeated.

"Explain," ordered Ryan.

Sam's face was hard—no easy-going grin, no teasing remarks. Only the soldier remained.

"Bethany Rose. She'll come here."

Bethany Rose was one of the Wolf Council's enforcers. She was a unique werewolf, able to sniff out magic and its users. The Council used her to track witches in the North and often killed them when they were found. They knew Esme was part of our Pack; Sam himself had managed to get a pardon for Esme when she helped us defeat Brock's army. But the conditions stipulated were that Esme was never to practice magic here again, on pain of death for her and any who helped her. I knew Esme had broken that rule a number of times, even suspected Jem was encouraging it, helping her to hone her skills and become a deadly fighter who could defend herself. But none of us would risk Esme being caught by the Council.

Jase frowned. "Why? The Council doesn't involve themselves in every little spat."

"True, but we have a lead on ripple." Sam swept his arm to point outside. "On some of the witches involved in ripple. This is now way bigger than one child. We've been chasing any leads on the witches involved for months. No matter what happens here with the Knox Pack, the Wolf Council will investigate. Bethany Rose will come; she'll be needed to track the witches."

Esme shifted closer to Jem, her hand brushing his arm.

"She'll know if Esme has used magic," Sam continued. "I won't be able to protect her this time. It'll be a death sentence. We can't use her."

"Esme stays out of this fight," Jem said, the low growl that rumbled from his chest reverberating through the room. It was a threat, directed at anyone who dared argue.

I saw Ryan's face go blank.

Uh-oh.

"Agreed," I said before Ryan and Jem got into another who's-the-fucking-Alpha argument that would push Jem further out of our Pack.

Esme threw both hands up in the air, rounding on Jem. "This! This is why I need to learn how to fight! I'm useless without my magic!"

"You're not useless." Jem's voice was firm. The fierceness in his usually hollow tone made everyone go still. "You're alive. And you'll stay alive."

"I can Shift," said Mason. "Go out the back. See if I can circle around and get eyes on them."

Ryan nodded. "Do it. Take Derek and Sam with you."

Mason cast a swift look at Shya and pressed a kiss to her forehead. "You'll—?"

"I'll protect the kids. Just be safe, okay?"

Mason nodded, then jerked his chin at Derek and Sam.

They moved as one, smooth, silent, and predatory, as they slipped out of the room. They might not have shared Pack bonds anymore, but they would always be Pack.

Esme's breath hitched, her eyes going wide. "They're here," she whispered.

Knock. Knock.

Everyone turned their heads to the front door.

None of us had heard them approach. There was nothing in my Pack bonds or my link to our territory that told me outsiders were here.

Esme was right. They had slipped past our carefully laid defenses undetected. They were playing with us.

Knock. Knock. Knock.

Well, wasn't that just fucking awesome.

CHAPTER EIGHTEEN

RYAN

They were fucking with us. My wolf growled inside of me.

Teach them a lesson.

I planned to.

"Stay inside," I ordered, then pointed at Jase. "Protect Lark."

He nodded as I strode to the door.

"Not without me." Mai stepped in my path.

I thought about picking her up, carrying her to the study, and tying her to the chair.

"Don't even think about it," she warned.

Right. She knew me and my wolf too well.

"First sign of trouble—"

"I'll protect me and the baby."

I didn't like it. No, scratch that, I fucking hated it. But this was the line my wolf and I trod with Mai. I'd spent months scared out of my mind that she would run again if I got too overprotective. Now, after what we had been through, I knew she wouldn't leave me, but I'd definitely be sleeping on the couch if I overstepped. She spent too many years thinking she was less capable than others, that she was weak because she had run when I'd rejected her, and ended up with an ex who beat the crap out of her. She wasn't weak; she was the strongest fucking person I had ever known. My job was to show her just how awesome she was, not put her down or make her think she was less in any way, and I was slowly learning to stretch my comfort zone of Mai situations where my wolf and I didn't go crazy with the need to protect her.

"Besides," said Mai, as if she could read my thoughts, "if the Knox Pack were going to attack, they would have done that by now; they wouldn't be knocking on our door."

Okay, she may have a point there.

"Fine, but stay behind me."

"Twelve hostiles," Waylen called, eyes on his screens. "About a hundred feet from the door. Spread out in a semi-circle on the lawn. Behind them, to the left of the Ancestral Fire, another two."

Esme stepped forward. "They'll be the witches. Watch their hands. Even the best sometimes will clench or twitch their fingers as they cast."

"Any others?" Mai asked Waylen.

He shook his head. "None that I can see. But apparently, that don't mean shit with witches involved."

We were going to need Waylen to spend the next few months working with Esme to see if he could make something that would see through the magic the witches cast to hide themselves and others. There was no fucking way witches were strolling into our territory again.

I swung the door open. Wally had done his magic here as well.

Twinkling lights wrapped around the trunks of the trees and between the branches. It looked like fireflies were flitting around our garden. Under the glittering lights, I could see twelve of them, spread out in a semi-circle—a careful formation, deliberate ... calculated. The Knox Pack. They were silent as I scanned them. Most of them were in their wolf forms, huge, hulking beasts with coats the color of shadows that shifted under the dim light of the porch.

Two figures in human form stood at the center—I was guessing this was Gabrielle and Artie. They were young, early-twenties at most, but there was nothing soft about them. Both had the lean, predatory look of wolves who'd fought their way to power. Gabrielle was standing tall, her posture stiff like a soldier on parade, in a dark maroon jacket, tight black pants, and leather boots that came up to her ankles. Her eyes, sharp and assessing, narrowed at the sight of us. Her hair was black and plaited into a high ponytail that didn't shift an inch in the biting wind as it raked across the porch. Artie was visibly more of a direct threat. His body was built for combat—broad shoulders, thick neck, and hard edges all over. Brown hair was cut short against his head. His nose, flat and wide, looked like it had been broken several times. There was no mistaking the tension flowing through him. He radiated it, his scarred knuckles clenching and unclenching at his sides like he had been half-hoping we'd give him an excuse to smash down the door. They were dangerous, yes, but my wolf wasn't concerned.

As I glanced at the Ancestral Fire, the flames sputtered, a warm shimmer against the cold night, casting shadows across the decorations—pines wrapped with ribbons, flickering lights hanging between the branches like stars. My eyes caught on the two humans standing behind the Knox Pack. They were dressed in warm winter clothes, woolen hats, scarves wrapped around their faces, fur-lined coats, and boots. Interestingly, no gloves. Werewolves felt the cold, but we weren't as bothered by it as humans or witches. Even if I couldn't smell that they weren't Shifters, the layers on these two would have told me that.

Well, hello there, witches.

The taller of the two, a woman with platinum blonde hair peeking out from under her hat, had a stern expression as she glared at our house. The other witch, a shorter man with a thin, lined face and crooked nose, stood with his arms folded, his jaw clenched as he scanned me and Mai. I could feel a subtle hum in the air around them, like static—magic, building slowly and deliberately.

"Please," the one I pegged as Gabrielle took a few steps forward, smiling without a trace of warmth. "We're not looking for a fight. My name is Gabrielle, and this is my mate Artie."

I forced my body to stay relaxed and frowned at her. "This your usual way of introducing yourselves? Rolling up with ten wolves in tow? Gotta say, I don't see you being invited to many parties."

She spread her hands out in a placating gesture. "I apologize for the show of force. They are simply here to help protect our pup on our journey back home. We have found traversing the territories of other Packs to be perilous."

No shit.

"This simplifies things," she continued, "both for us and for those who may wish to do us harm."

I bet it did.

"What exactly can we do for you?"

"We appreciate you taking care of our pup, but we're here to bring her home where she belongs."

"Your pup?" asked Mai, feigning ignorance.

Gabrielle smiled again. "Yes. The girl. Lark. She is part of our Pack. I'm sure you know what it is like when you have been separated from a member of your Pack? The lengths you'll go to to make sure they return safely."

Nice. The threat there was subtle.

"Lark is safe here. She's made it clear she doesn't want to return to your Pack."

Artie's jaw clenched. "She's a child. She doesn't get to make that decision."

Gabrielle whipped her head around to stare at her mate. He lowered his eyes. She was in charge and she didn't want him to do the speaking. Interesting.

She turned back to us, and this time, the softness in Gabrielle's expression hardened just a touch. "Lark is confused. I don't know if she told you, but her parents recently died. It was a tragic accident. Lark is struggling. We—her Pack—are the only ones who can give her the support and protection she needs. You can understand that, can't you? Caring for your own?"

Her words were meant to disarm, to sound reasonable. We're just a friendly Pack looking after our pups.

Mai's lips twitched. "Were you caring for your own when you forced Lark's parents to take ripple?"

Artie's eyes darkened, his fingers clenching and unclenching faster now, but Gabrielle—Gabrielle didn't flinch. She just took another step forward.

"As I said, the girl is confused. To lose her family at such a young age is devastating. I suspect she overheard things that upset her, things that she doesn't understand, things that she has twisted in her head to mean something it is not. She's a lost, confused child. The sooner she is back with us, and we get this all cleared up, the happier she will be. Will you really stand in the way of that? I'm sure you want to resolve this peacefully and don't want us to get the Wolf Council involved?"

Mai quirked an eyebrow at me. Yeah, the Knox Pack hadn't done their homework. It must have worked for them in the past. Roll up, threaten to involve the Wolf Council, and they get whatever they want. I'd heard of this tactic being used successfully against smaller Packs, especially those that didn't want any trouble, in order for a roaming Pack to steal supplies and food. But we weren't a small Pack; we knew how to deal with trouble, and we had a fucking member of the Wolf Council sneaking up behind them right now.

"Oh, I don't know," I drawled lazily. "Sounds like making your Pack members take ripple, getting them addicted, and then killing them might be something the Wolf Council would be real interested in."

"Fuck this!" Artie spat, then whirled to the witches behind him. "She's in there, and these fuckers know too much. You need to deal with them."

"Agreed." The female witch's voice was smooth and cold as she stepped around the wolves and walked toward the house. "I was hoping we could do this cleanly. But it seems you've gone snooping where you don't belong."

Mai tensed next to me, and I knew she felt it too, the electric build-up of magic. The witch was gathering her power.

"Now, unfortunately, it's going to get messy."

She lifted her hand, her fingers twisting gracefully in the cold air.

Fuck! I ripped my top off and let the change take me. My bones cracked and reformed with frightening speed, the sound like branches snapping in a storm. Muscles rippled and bulged beneath my skin, which stretched and darkened as thick, midnight fur erupted across my body. The power of the Dark Goddess surged through me like lightning, making the transformation almost instantaneous. My jaw extended with a series of sickening pops, teeth lengthening into deadly fangs as my face reshaped into a lupine muzzle. In seconds, I towered nine feet tall, a primal force of muscle, claw, and fang.

The witch's wrist flicked with a snap as though tearing a string from the fabric of the world itself. I spun to Mai, reaching out with clawed hands large enough to crush a man's skull as a violent gust crashed into us both, lifting our bodies high off the porch and flinging us in opposite directions.

"Mai!"

The edges of the world spun, a whirlwind of snow, glittering fairy lights, and Mai's frightened face as she flew away from me.

Chapter Nineteen

Mai

I landed hard in the snow, instinctively curling inwards to protect my baby. A white-hot jolt of pain shot through my arm, but it didn't matter. Not right now. Anger rolled through me. The witch had tossed us aside like we were stick men.

Fuck, no!

This was no longer about just protecting Lark. We were the Three Rivers Pack, and we submitted to no one.

I pushed myself to my feet and saw my wolves—my family—on the attack. From different corners of the compound, Sam, Derek, and Mason sprinted, huge and snarling, toward the attacking Pack and their witches. The front door swung open, and Jem, Jase, Sofia, Esme, Wally, Maxwell, Amara, and Cameron poured out.

My eyes sought out Ryan, and there he was in his True Werewolf form. Absolutely massive, dwarfing the regular wolves of the Knox Pack. His dark fur rippled with power as snow fell softly around him. He looked like something out of legend, a myth come to life, as he let out an almighty roar full of rage.

The Knox Pack instinctively cringed away, their movements

faltering. I recognized their shock. You couldn't see Ryan's True Werewolf form and not hesitate.

I moved, adrenaline pumping through my veins. My foot kicked against the soft snow as I launched forward. One of the wolves—a big one with dark, mottled fur streaked with gray—turned just as I crashed into him. Before he could snap at me, I wrapped my arm around his muzzle and used my momentum to drive him to the ground. His neck twisted to the side as we fell, and I used my other hand to deliver three punches in quick succession to his throat. He collapsed under me, and I jumped up, looking for my next target. My breath fogged in the cold air as I saw him.

Ryan.

Carving a path through the Knox Pack straight to me. Behind him, four werewolves were crumpled on the ground in various states of consciousness. He reached me, and his strong arms pulled me to him.

"Safe," he growled.

Yes. I was safe. The baby was safe. He was safe. But he was interrupting me kicking ass.

I pulled back. "We're okay!"

I saw in his eyes, felt it in our mate bond, his plan. He was going to take me out of here, get me to safety before coming back to fight.

"Don't you dare!" I warned.

This was just like in my nightmares. Ryan's attention on me, on the baby, leaving the rest of our Pack vulnerable. They'd fall while Ryan tried to protect me. Just the thought of it brought me out in a cold sweat.

"Ryan!" I snapped, yanking my arm free from his grasp.

Out of the corner of my eye I saw a flash of silver fur barrel through the field of snow. One of the Knox wolves—stocky, with blazing yellow eyes—charged at Ryan's blindside. He turned to intercept, but he wasn't fast enough.

"No!"

I lunged forward just as Ryan lifted me out of the way with one arm, as he literally stomped on the wolf, his foot coming down on the wolf's head and driving it into the snow.

Alrighty then.

To our left, there were snarls and yelps of pain as my Pack attacked.

Sofia threw knives with deadly accuracy. Two of them caught one of the Knox wolves in the shoulder, and it stumbled back with a yelp.

Maxwell moved with a lethal grace I hadn't expected from a human. He leaped, sailing over an approaching werewolf, twisted in mid-air, and as he landed, drove his knee into the wolf's head.

Amara and Cameron fought side by side, their movements synchronized as they tag-teamed a large gray wolf. Cameron ducked as Amara jumped over him, her compact white wolf a blur of teeth as she slammed into their opponent.

Wally charged forward, his tennis racket held high like a sword, his battle cry ringing out across the snowy lawn. "This is for ruining my decorations, bitches!"

Ryan froze next to me, and I whirled to him. He was straining, his face tight with tension, muscles bugling.

What the hell?

"Can't. Move," he said through gritted teeth.

The witches. They were targeting Ryan as the biggest threat.

I spun, seeking them out. Near the edge of the battle, Esme was throwing snowballs at the witches. The snowballs were dissolving mid-air before they could hit their targets.

What was she doing?

We need to distract them, Esme's voice rang in my mind. *There's a limit to the spells they can cast.*

If we concentrated our attacks on the witches, they'd have to focus on fending us off, and maybe Ryan could break free.

Tell the others, I ordered Esme. She could speak in their minds and it meant we didn't give our tactics away.

"Jem, Jase, cover us!" I yelled. We'd need someone protecting our backs.

From the right, I saw Sam lunge at the male witch. He flicked his hand to the side, and Sam bounced off an invisible barrier. Derek sailed over Sam's head, trying to go over the barrier, but he hit it too and crashed to the ground.

One of Sofia's knives hurtled past me, heading straight for the blonde. A gust of wind caught it and flung it back toward her.

I didn't think so.

I plucked it out of the air as it sailed past. I was still twenty feet from her.

Behind me, I heard Ryan's roar. It was working.

Derek and Sam were throwing themselves against the barrier. Sprinting, I threw the knife at the male witch's back. He sensed it coming and waved his arm, but it was too late. The knife sliced the side of his face as he turned. Blood ran down his cheek, and the barrier broke. Derek and Sam surged through, and the witch disappeared under their huge bodies.

I didn't stop. I focused on the blonde. She whirled to face me as snowballs from all sides zoomed toward her. Maxwell, Sofia, Shya,

Esme, and Wally were scooping up snow and launching them at the witch. One after the other.

Ten feet.

A Knox wolf appeared on my left. It's jaw wide, ready to tear my flesh, it darted in. I braced for impact, but suddenly Jem was there, his body slamming into the attacking wolf, another one of Sofia's knives in his hand. For a split second, our eyes met, and I saw it—a flash of my brother, my protector, the one who'd taught me how to fight, who'd held me when our parents died.

Then Jem punched the blade into the wolf's side, two, three, five times. It was quick and brutal, efficient.

"Go," he growled, the word rough with effort. "I've got your back."

I kept going.

Five feet.

The witch was batting the snowballs away. Behind her, I saw Wally reach into his cargo pants and pull out two tennis balls.

Three feet.

He threw the first one up in the air, swung the tennis racket and executed a perfect serve. The ball careered straight for her. Her fingers twitched and the ball dropped out of the sky. The snowball Esme had thrown at the same time slammed into her stomach though.

Gotcha.

She took one step back, and I crashed into her. She was ready for me and twisted with her hips, using my momentum to send me smacking into the snow. I rolled and was on my feet in an instant. Another tennis ball whacked into the back of her head as I charged. I leaned forward, my shoulder ramming into her midriff, and wrapped my arms around her legs. I pulled, taking her feet from under her. Her back and head slammed into the ground with a satisfying crack. I scrambled up and wedged a knee on her throat as Maxwell appeared by my side, grabbing her wrists so she couldn't perform any more spells.

With the witches down, the fight turned chaotic—claws tearing, fangs snapping, knives whirling through the air. The snow beneath our feet turned pink with blood. Through it all, Ryan stayed too close, his massive form constantly shifting to keep himself between me and any threat. Every time I tried to engage, he was there, blocking, protecting, when we both needed to be fighting.

My attention snapped back to Ryan as another wolf lunged for us. This time, I wasn't going to let him handle it alone. I ducked under Ryan's protective stance and met the attack head-on, driving my knee up into the wolf's chest. The impact sent shockwaves through my leg, but the wolf yelped and stumbled back.

"Mai!" Ryan's growl was filled with frustration as he moved to shield me again.

No. This couldn't happen. We wouldn't lose anyone because he was too focused on protecting me.

A blur of dark brown fur streaked past the front door—Lark. The small wolf's eyes blazed with hatred as she launched herself at Artie, teeth bared for his throat. My heart stopped. She was too small, too young—

"Lark, no!" I screamed, but my voice was lost in the chaos.

Ryan's attention snapped to the pup, his protective instincts warring between me and the child in danger. To my left, Derek took a brutal hit to his side, knocked off balance as his opponent capitalized on his split-second glance in my direction. The Knox wolf's teeth dug into his shoulder, and crimson bloomed across the snow.

Artie caught Lark mid-leap, his larger form easily subduing her. She thrashed wildly, her fury giving her strength beyond her size, but she was no match for an adult wolf. My stomach lurched as I moved to help her.

Ryan grabbed me and pulled me back. Ahead, a massive black wolf slammed into Mason, driving him backward into a tree. The impact shook snow from the branches above and sent it falling over them both.

Sam's opponent got past his guard, and claws raked across his flank, and he barely managed to roll away from a follow-up attack that would have torn out his throat.

This was my nightmare come to life. Ryan trying to protect me, leaving the rest of our Pack vulnerable.

"Cam!"

I turned as Amara's voice called out sharp with warning. A Knox wolf separated them, driving Amara back while another circled behind Cameron.

I spun away from Ryan, desperate to help, to fight, to do something. But my movement had been anticipated. A clawed hand curled around my neck, cutting off oxygen, and yanked me back.

"Stop!" Gabrielle yelled, her voice loud in my ear. "Stop, or I'll kill her!"

Chapter Twenty

MAI

Everyone froze.

My eyes went to Ryan's. His massive form vibrated with barely contained fury, desperate to take action but knowing if he made a move, he would kill me and our baby. The rage there was absolute, primal—his True Werewolf form seeming to grow even larger as his muscles bunched, preparing to tear Gabrielle apart. But he didn't move. None of them did. The entire Three Rivers Pack had gone completely still.

Gabrielle's claws dug into my throat, drawing tiny pinpricks of blood. "I mean it," she snarled. "Everyone back off. We got what we came for. No one else needs to die."

I wasn't buying that for a second. They would use me and Lark to capture the others, then kill us all. They couldn't afford to leave any witnesses alive.

"Let the witch go," Artie ordered, his hands clamped tight over Lark's muzzle. Her eyes rolled with hatred as she squirmed beneath him, but he held her fast.

I could smell the satisfaction rolling off Gabrielle in waves. Through our mate bond, I felt Ryan's struggle, and it was the same as mine—fear, cold as steel, slicing along the bond, with the overwhelming urge to protect warring with the tactical need to wait for an opening.

Ryan nodded at Maxwell, and he released the blonde. The male witch was unconscious, his body a mess of bloody gashes, slowly leaking into the surrounding snow.

The blonde's voice cut through the silence. "Well, well. Looks like we found their weakness." She stepped forward, her boots crunching in the bloodied snow. "All that power and you let it fall apart the moment someone threatens your Alpha."

We are not weak. My wolf snarled inside me.

Damn fucking right, we weren't.

"Face it," Gabrielle panted as she swiped blood from a claw mark above her right eye. "You lost. Be smart now and minimize the damage while you still can. Stand down. We'll take Lark and release your Alpha when we get to your borders."

Ryan's face was blank, but I could see in his eyes that he was considering all the angles, trying to find one that kept me and our baby alive.

My mind flashed to Lark's face as she'd told us about her family—the pain, the loss, the betrayal by her own Alphas. For fuck's sake, she thought she was safer with a biker gang than a Pack now. Rage surged through me. No. We'd promised to protect her, and we would keep that promise. Ryan had warned me not to make rash decisions. I knew it was my temper and my hormones pushing me to act, but Sofia was right; I had to trust my instincts. They were all I had left right now.

Lark went completely limp in Artie's grasp.

Shit! We were out of time.

"No deal," I snarled despite the claws at my throat.

Gabrielle's grip tightened. "You don't get a say in this."

I laughed, the sound harsh and cold. "I'm the fucking Alpha of the Three Rivers Pack. I always get a say."

I felt Ryan's sharp attention focus on me. He knew that tone. Knew what it meant. I was done playing nice.

I looked back at my beautiful Ryan. In that moment, something passed between us—he knew what I was going to do. He gave me the barest of nods.

I smiled.

Then I moved.

I drove my elbow back into Gabrielle's solar plexus, simultaneously dropping my weight and twisting. Her claws raked my neck as I broke free, but I barely felt it. My wolf surged forward, lending me her strength as I spun and slammed my fist into her jaw.

Out of the corner of my eye, I saw Artie loosen his hold on Lark. The moment his grip slackened, Lark twisted violently, her small form writhing like an eel. Her teeth found his hand, and she bit down hard. Artie howled, instinctively releasing her, then stumbled back.

The battlefield erupted.

The witch's spell hit me like a freight train, sending me sprawling into the snow. Pain exploded through my side, but I tucked and rolled. Behind me, I heard Ryan's earth-shattering snarl as he finally had the opening he needed.

Ryan burst into motion, his massive True Werewolf form crossing the distance in a single bound. The witch raised her hands, magic crackling, but she was a fraction too slow. Ryan's massive paw caught her square in the chest, sending her flying backward into a tree with a sickening crunch.

I scrambled to my feet, one hand protectively curved around my stomach. Blood trickled down my neck from Gabrielle's claws, but my wolf was singing with fierce joy. We were free to fight now, and my Pack no longer had to hold back.

Gabrielle screamed in rage as she charged toward me. Another of Sofia's knives—just how many did she have?— found her thigh, throwing her off balance. I met her attack head-on, ducking under her swinging arm and driving my knee into her ribs. I heard the sound of bones cracking.

Through it all, I could feel Ryan's attention on me—not suffocating now, but watchful, coordinated. We moved together, fought together, protecting each other while letting each other fight. This was how it should be. Not him shielding me, but us working as one.

To my left I saw Lark, creeping up behind Artie, who was still cursing and clutching his bleeding hand. He turned at the last second and saw her. Artie braced himself, but Lark had learned. Instead of going for a direct attack, she feinted left, then ducked right, her teeth catching his ankle. He stumbled, trying to shake her off.

"You little—" he snarled, but his words cut off as Maxwell appeared behind him.

Maxwell's fist connected with Artie's jaw in a precise strike that rocked the werewolf back. As Artie staggered, Lark released his ankle and launched herself at his chest. The combination of her momentum and Maxwell's punch sent Artie sprawling into the snow. Before he could recover, Lark was on him, her teeth at his throat, a low growl rumbling from her small frame.

I turned to see that the Knox Pack members who could still move were retreating, dragging their unconscious Packmates with them. One witch lay crumpled at the base of the tree where Ryan had thrown her, and the other was pinned beneath Sam's wolf, bleeding heavily.

Gabrielle staggered backward, clutching her broken ribs. Her eyes darted between her fallen Pack members, the witches, and us. The calculation on her face was clear—they had lost badly, and now she was weighing her options.

"It's over," I said, my voice carrying across the blood-stained snow. "Surrender now."

As one, Ryan, Mason, Derek, Sam, and Maxwell turned to stare at Gabrielle. A low rumble came from Ryan's throat. He wanted her to say no, wanted the chance to get revenge for all the Knox Pack had done. Derek and Sam stalked forward, their eyes locked on their prey. Gabrielle wasn't stupid. Her shoulders slumped as she held out her hands.

"Fine," she said through gritted teeth. "We surrender."

I nodded to Derek and Mason, who moved to secure the prisoners. As they did, I felt Ryan behind me, his massive form radiating heat in the cold night air. Through our bond, I could feel his pride, his relief, and his love washing over me.

Behind us, Wally's voice rang out cheerfully, "So, who wants hot chocolate? I don't know about you, but I find there is nothing like a post-battle sugar rush!"

Chapter Twenty-One

MAI

The fire crackled as I settled onto the couch, watching Lark fidget with the hem of her sweater. It was nearly midnight. Wally had found a Christmas playlist on his music streaming app, and Mariah Carey's "All I Want for Christmas" was playing on the speakers Ryan had installed around the house.

I glanced around, my eyes automatically drawn to the Christmas tree that could have graced the lobby of a five-star hotel. Strings of warm white lights were expertly woven through the lush boughs, creating a soft, romantic glow. Mercury glass ornaments and glistening icicle ornaments hung artfully, catching the firelight like prisms.

When I first walked in here, after cleaning up after the fight, and seen the shimmery ribbons, beaded garlands, and twinkling lights draped along every surface, Wally had thrown his arms out, and asked me what I thought. I'd said the first thing that had come to mind. "It's very...um...sparkly."

Wally had grinned. "Good. You can never have too much sparkle, honey."

Now, taking in the sleek metallic bows and lustrous winterberry wreaths that he'd added to the mantle, and sculpted reindeer figurines in the corners that peeked out from amidst the mounds of pearlescent-beaded garlands draped to look like glistening snowdrifts, I wondered at how Wally had managed, despite the chaos of today, to transform our Alpha House into a winter wonderland for everyone.

It was exactly what we all needed after the events of this evening. After the fight, Thomas and Amara had patched everyone up, the Knox Pack and witches had been secured in the enforcers building—Sam would be taking them to the kennel, the name most Shifters gave the Adarcan Prison, tomorrow.

The surviving prospect had finally caught up with Ronnie, and he'd called his brother. Maxwell had walked off into the forest to have that conversation without all of us hearing, though we'd had to cover the kids' ears, given the yelling and language, before he was out of earshot. Maxwell had returned fifteen minutes later to say that Ronnie would be here in the morning. After that, I'd announced that it was finally time for Ben's Birthday Christmas celebrations. Sylvie was busy putting the last touches to the meal and had shooed us all out of the kitchen. Everyone except Maxwell, which was interesting. I was going to have to find out more about him.

Lark had been quiet since the fight ended. Some of the tension had left her, but her scent told me she was feeling wary and uncertain.

"Lark," I said softly, "we need to talk about what happens next."

She jutted out her chin and glared up at me. "I'm staying with Ronnie. You can't stop me!"

I was pretty sure if we tried to keep her here, she would run away the first chance she got. If Ronnie was just using her to get information, I would kill him myself. "You don't have to go anywhere you don't want to. But we do need to deal with your bonds to the Knox Pack."

"I don't want any Pack bonds," she said, her voice sharp with fear. "Packs are stupid."

"Not all Packs are like the Knox Pack. Being part of a Pack is about strength in numbers; it's about protecting each other and having someone to look out for you," I explained. "But more than that, Pack bonds help ground us; they help our wolves stay balanced and healthy. Without them, we can become unstable, dangerous to ourselves and others."

She considered this, her fingers still worrying at her sweater. "I … I don't want to hurt Ronnie. Does that mean I have to keep the bonds?"

I shook my head. "Not if you don't want to. I can teach you how to break your Knox Pack bonds. But after that, you'll need new ones."

Her face scrunched up. "You mean, stay here? Be part of your Pack?"

"We need to talk to Ronnie about it, work out all the details, but maybe there is a way for you to stay with him."

Hope bloomed in her eyes. "Really?"

"Really. But it would come with conditions."

She narrowed her eyes at me. "What sort of conditions?"

"Well, for starters, you'd need to visit us at least twice a month, plus the three days around the full moon. That way, your Pack bonds would stay healthy, and you can learn about being a werewolf. You're about to hit your teenage years; that means lots of change is coming, and you need to know how to deal with it all."

"And when I'm here, I can borrow your books?"

I smiled. "Anytime."

"And I wouldn't need to leave Ronnie? I could live with him?"

Ronnie really meant something to her; that much was clear. "Being part of our Pack doesn't mean giving up your found family—it means adding to it."

Lark seemed to consider this carefully, her eyes darting to where Ben and Tucker were setting up dominos under the Christmas tree. The twinkling lights cast a warm glow over their faces as they argued about the rules.

"Would I get to play with them when I came to visit?"

"Of course. That's part of being in our Pack—there'll always be some Packmates around to play with."

Ben looked up then. "Hey, Lark! Come help! Tucker's trying to cheat!"

"Am not!" Tucker gave Ben a playful shove.

Lark glanced at me, seeking permission. I nodded, and she scrambled off the couch, racing over to join them under the glittering tree.

Around the room, my Pack was settling into the celebration. Mason had pulled Shya onto his lap in the oversized armchair, his fingers absently playing with her hair as they watched the kids play. She smiled and leaned back into him, completely at ease in his arms.

Near the fireplace, Amara was attempting to hang more tinsel while Cameron kept trying to "help," which mostly involved wrapping the sparkly strands around her instead of the mantle.

"You're doing it wrong," he teased, pulling her closer with the tinsel.

"Oh, really?" She raised an eyebrow at him. "And you're the tinsel expert now?"

"I'm an expert at making you smile," he replied and pressed a kiss to her nose.

Behind them, from his spot by the door, Jase pretended to gag.

Maxwell appeared from the kitchen with a tray of hot chocolate, Sylvie's scent mingling with his. I suppressed a smile. I had a feeling I knew exactly what they'd been doing in there.

"You missed a spot," Sofia called out, pointing to where Derek was attempting to rehang some fallen Christmas lights.

Derek turned, the muscles in his arms flexing as he stretched to reach the lights. "If you're such an expert," he drawled, his eyes darkening as they swept over her, "why don't you come up here and show me how it's done?"

Sofia's heart rate picked up—something every wolf in the room could hear.

"Because then who would protect these candy canes from becoming Wally's latest 'artistic inspiration'?" She gestured to where Wally was attempting to create what he called a "candy cane Christmas tree sculpture" that looked more like something from a horror movie.

"I'm creating art!" Wally declared, waving around a half-melted candy cane. "This will be my masterpiece—'Christmas Joy in Red and White.' Or possibly 'Santa's Revenge.' I haven't decided yet."

I watched as Derek's eyes stayed locked on Sofia. The way he tracked her movements reminded me of how Ryan used to watch me before we got together—like a predator waiting for the perfect moment to pounce.

A sudden blur of motion caught my eye as Ben launched himself off the floor towards Wally. The room seemed to still, everyone holding their breath as Ben tackled Wally in a fierce hug. "This is the best birthday ever!" he cried, his voice muffled against Wally's shirt.

You could have heard a pin drop. We all knew how much this meant to Wally—to throw the perfect party, to make Ben's first birthday celebration as part of Wally and Thomas' family one he would never forget. Wally's arms tightened almost convulsively around the boy, and his shoulders shook ever so slightly.

"It was no problem at all, Ben! You deserved it!" Wally choked out, one hand flailing up to dab under his eyes.

Ben looked up at Wally. "Are you...are you crying?" A horrified expression formed on Ben's face. "Did I make you cry?"

"I am not crying, you hear me? I'm just...sweating through my eyes. From all the party planning exertion! It's a completely normal thing."

A wave of soft laughter rippled through the room. Thomas grinned as he made his way over, put his arm around Wally and ruffled Ben's hair.

"Better get used to it, Ben," Thomas said gruffly. "Wally's eyes tend to sweat a lot!"

I stood up, smiling, and felt Ryan's strong arms slide around my waist from behind. "Dance with me?"

I raised my eyebrows. "Dance. Me?"

"You'll be great; just follow my lead."

He pulled me against his chest, and I relaxed into his warmth, swaying to the music.

"You did good with Lark," he murmured, pressing a kiss to my temple.

I nodded as he spun me slowly around the room. In the corner, Sam was having an intense debate about "Star Wars" with Waylen, who was gesturing wildly with a half-eaten gingerbread wolf.

By the tree, Esme skipped over to the children. "Can I play? I'm good at dominoes, and I promise I won't cheat for the first five minutes."

Jem, leaning against the far wall with his arms crossed, smiled. It flashed across his face, there and gone before I'd blinked, but I saw it. I had thought they would leave after the battle, but they had stuck around.

"How are you doing? You seem calmer."

I knew Ryan wasn't asking about the fight, and he was right. I did feel calmer. I didn't know if I would always get it right, but I trusted my instincts. I'd take it one day at a time, one challenge at a time, and would do the best I could. Ryan and me were in for one hell of an adventure, but we would figure it out.

"I feel calmer. I don't think I'm going to be having more nightmares."

His eyebrow shot up. "Really? You finally gonna tell me what they were about?"

I sighed and bit my bottom lip. "I...I was scared that in the middle of a fight, you would be too focused on protecting me, and ... and that someone in our Pack would die because of it."

He leaned down and whispered in my ear. "You will always come first."

"I know. But you trusted me back there. In those moments when Gabrielle had me, you trusted that I would get me and the baby out of it. I know that now. You didn't see me as weak and in need of help. You saw me, Ryan. You knew I was capable of doing it."

"I'm not gonna lie and say it didn't kill me out there, and I'm never not gonna want to destroy anyone who threatens you, but you're more than capable of protecting both you and our kids. I'm glad you know it, too."

I nodded. "I finally realized that me giving a shit is not a weakness. It makes me who I am. It makes me a better leader, a better Alpha, and it makes our Pack stronger."

Ryan grinned. "You know, I think you're the last in the Pack to work that out."

"The last one, huh?"

"Yes!" Wally, Sofia, Jase, and Derek all called at the same time.

Okay, then.

Ryan kept us dancing, leading us into the hallway. "I have a present for you."

"You got me a present?"

"Three presents, actually. I've been trying to talk to you all day about the first one. I'm going to build you a cabin. In the forest. Still in the Three Rivers, but away from the town and anyone who might be tempted to disturb us. Say with questions about tinsel emergency protocols."

My breath caught. "A cabin? For us? Just us?"

"I thought we could do with a place to escape to once in a while. Just for you and me. Not Alphas Mai and Ryan, just you and your brother's best friend who has loved you your entire life. But only if you want it."

I felt my eyes well up. Want it? It was the most thoughtful gift anyone had ever gotten me.

"Ryan, it sounds absolutely perfect."

He smiled and twirled me further down the corridor. "Good. That takes us to present number two."

"You don't need—"

"Don't even try. I'm going to get you as many presents as I want. And, here's letting you in on a little secret, they won't be just at birthdays or Christmas, they're gonna be all the time."

"Ryan—"

"Present number two," he interrupted. "I talked with Jem."

I frowned, knowing where this was going. "I know; Esme told me what happened last week. I love that you tried, but Jem isn't ready to spend time with me. I'll find a way to be alright with that."

"Uh-huh. Did Esme tell you I talked to Jem again?"

I shook my head, hoping Ryan hadn't made it worse with Jem; they'd been best friends for so long.

"He's agreed to come over for Friday night dinners. Him and Esme. As a trial run at first, but I'll be there, and I'd never let him hurt you. Plus, Esme is handy with her magic these days. She'll hit him with a spell if his wolf gets out of control."

I stood still, not able to move, and just looked at Ryan.

"No more dancing?" he teased.

I didn't reply. I couldn't. Tears rolled down my cheeks.

"Mai—"

"You...he...you!"

His expression turned worried. "I can tell him not to come—"

"Don't you dare!" I pointed my finger accusingly at him. "He really said he'd come?"

"Yes."

"Oh my Goddess, Ryan!" I leapt, flinging myself into his arms. He caught me, his strong arms wrapping round me as he held me tight. "Thank you! You've given my brother back to me."

I felt his chest rumble as he chuckled. "It's just dinner but it's a start."

"I can't...this means so much to me, Ryan. I thought I'd lost him for good."

He set me down on my feet, wiping my tears away with his thumbs. "I'll do anything to make you happy, Mai. Anything. Which brings me to present number three."

"No more presents, Ryan! Really. You've given me everything I could have ever wanted. You gave me you, this Pack, this family, and now my brother back."

"There will always be more, Mai." His smile turned dark as he slipped his arms round my waist and started dancing again. "This present is for later, though, when I've kicked everyone out of here."

"So, in what? Five minutes?" I teased.

He frowned, then spun me, twirling me out and pulling me close. "I'll give them till after dinner. Then our no-one-in-our-vicinity days begin. I have plans."

A warmth spread through my chest. "Those plans better include us in bed."

"In bed, in the gym, in the lounge, in the kitchen, and the study. I told you, I have plans. Big plans. All night plans."

Er, yum!

"Maybe we send everyone home for dessert?"

He grinned down at me. "Whatever my Alpha wants."

His hand, hot against my back, slipped down, his fingers grazing the top of my ass, and I could feel my breasts tighten at just the thought of what he was going to do to me later.

"You know," Ryan said thoughtfully, "I could get used to this whole Christmas birthday thing."

"Really? The famously stubborn Ryan Shaw, accepting change?"

He grinned down at me. "Well, some changes are worth it."

Mate. Happy.

Yes, I said back to my wolf. We were happy.

"How's the little one doing? Still hungry?"

I placed my hand on my stomach as it gurgled as if on cue. "It's always hungry. I swear, if I didn't know better, I'd think it was a litter."

"Not a litter. Just twins."

I blinked up at him. "What?"

"Twins. I can hear their heartbeats."

I swayed, and Ryan caught me.

Just like I knew he always would.

What's next in Shifters of the Three Rivers? The Reluctant Mate. A Derek and Sofia story, coming 2025!

How far would you go for a second chance? Preorder now!

Want to know what happened on Derek and Sofia's hot and dangerous first date? Sign up to my newsletter at www.kiranightingale.com for a *free* prequel novella!

FREE BOOK! COME JOIN US IN THE SHIFTER REALM!

Kira Nightingale

Mystically Dark, Wildly Romantic...

Sign up to my newsletter and get Fairground Fling, a free prequel short story about Derek and Sofia's first date!

As an author, I write paranormal romance books that are mystically dark and wildly romantic. I send out my newsletter every week, and in it you can get exclusive content and snippets from my current work-in-progress, news about what I'm up to, and sometimes even photos of my clumsy cat, Scout. You can sign up to my newsletter at www.kiranightingale.com

Fairground Fling, Shifters of the Three Rivers 0.5

No way will I let fate decide my destiny, but Derek Shaw is back and proving impossible to resist

Sofia

All I wanted was to run my coffee shop in peace, avoid my fated mate, and forget about our Shifter bond. Is that too much to ask for?

Apparently it is, because Derek Shaw just walked back into my life, all rippling muscles and piercing eyes. The man sets my blood on fire, but there's no way I'm giving in. I've seen what happens when "fated mates" are torn apart, and I won't let that happen to me.

Derek left to join the military, turning his back on our bond. Now he's back in the Three Rivers Pack, determined to win me over. But I've built walls around my heart that even an Alpha wolf can't break through. At least, that's what I keep telling myself...

Derek

I left Three Rivers to serve my country, but I never forgot Sofia. Every day, her fiery hair and captivating scent haunted my thoughts.

Now I'm back, and the pull towards Sofia is stronger than ever. My wolf won't rest until I claim what's mine. But Sofia's determined to keep her distance. That's okay, though. I'm a Shaw, and we never back down from a challenge.

ALSO BY KIRA NIGHTINGALE

Shifters of the Three Rivers series

The Runaway Mate

The Renegade Mate

The Resolute Mate

The Rescued Mate

The Reluctant Mate(coming 2025)

The Relentless Mate (coming 2025)

A Three Rivers Holiday Tale: A Shifters of the Three Rivers Novella

Boxsets

Shifters of the Three Rivers, Omnibus of Books 1-3 (ebook only)

Mai and Ryan's story with *an exclusive epilogue!*

Audiobooks

The Runaway Mate (available on Audible and Amazon)

Coming Soon

The Renegade Mate
The Resolute Mate

ABOUT KIRA NIGHTINGALE

Kira Nightingale is a Scot living in Canada. She has always wanted to be a writer, and can't believe how lucky she is to finally be able to write romance stories all day long. She lives with her husband, her two children and a massive cat called Scout. Kira loves to drink tea (her favorite is Long Island Iced Tea, but unfortunately she only gets to drink this occasionally) and likes to dunk cookies in it (yes, even the Long Island kind.)

ACKNOWLEDGEMENTS

This novella is a thank you to my readers! I wanted to create a fun escape for everyone who has been so supportive and enthusiastic about my characters. You guys rock! I couldn't have done this without you.

I'd like to thank my wonderful editor, Brigitte Billings. Any mistakes are mine. The incredible cover was created by 100 Covers – thank you Jamie Ty for all your help and support.